THE MAPMAKER'S MONSTERS

BEWARE THE BUFFALOGRE!

Rob Stevens is a captain with a major British airline and does much of his writing in hotel rooms around the world. He grew up in Bournemouth and graduated from Cambridge University with a degree in engineering before training to be a pilot. He lives on the Dorset coast with his wife and two young sons.

Look out for more from THE MAPMAKER'S MONSTERS!

THE MAPMAKER'S MONSTERS

BEWARE THE BUFFALOGRE!

Rob Stevens

Illustrated by Adam Stower

MACMILLAN CHILDREN'S BOOKS

First published 2009 by Macmillan Children's Books
a division of Macmillan Publishers Limited
20 New Wharf Road, London N1 9RR
Basingstoke and Oxford
Associated companies throughout the world
www.panmacmillan.com

ISBN 978-0-330-45669-2

1 3 5 7 9 8 6 4 2

A CIP catalogue record for this book is available from
the British Library.

Typeset by Intype Libra Limited
Printed and bound in the UK by CPI Mackays, Chatham ME5 8TD

For Clare, Dylan and Charlie,
with all my heart

Prologue

'What on—?'

Pedro was confused and scared. What was happening to him? He had been feeling powerful, moving swiftly across the terrain, but suddenly he could barely stand. When he looked down he understood.

His pockets had filled with jewels, which were spilling on to the ground and piling up around his feet. A Roman centurion's helmet had appeared on his head and an ornate breastplate was clamped firmly round his body. An endless gold chain was coiling itself so tightly round his neck he could hardly breathe. If he didn't do something soon, he would be buried alive.

'Typical. I finally obtain my heart's desire and it tries to kill me.'

Pedro prised off the helmet and armour, unwound the chain and emptied his pockets. He found the small object he was looking for, dug a hole in the ground, pushed it in – along with the treasure – and covered the whole lot with earth. Glancing at the surrounding landscape, he scratched some markings on a small piece of wood and slipped it into his tunic. He would return with an army of men to reclaim what was his.

'What was that?!'

Twenty minutes later, Pedro was running for his life. He crashed through the forest, branches clawing at him, scratching his face and hands. Something was following him, and he wasn't waiting to find out what.

Now he could hear snorting. The ground thundered with the rhythm of galloping hoofs. Every now and then there was a terrifying screech that made Pedro shudder. It was getting closer.

Pedro burst out of the forest and sprinted across the uneven, stony ground towards the top of the cliff. The moon lit up his breath as it poured from his mouth and billowed into the sky.

Muscles aching, he reached the clifftop and glanced back. A shadowy shape emerged from the woods. It was an animal of some sort – charging towards him on all fours. The beast had thick, powerful shoulders. Its head hung low as it galloped. Four more animals came from within the trees, then another six. They were hunting as a pack and moving fast.

'Wonderful. That's just brilliant,' Pedro muttered angrily. He ran to an egg-shaped boulder and grabbed the rope that was coiled beneath it. He tossed it over the cliff and watched it unwind as it dropped silently to the beach below.

Holding the rope firmly in his hands, he walked

backwards over the cliff edge. Now only his toes were touching solid ground and there was nothing but sea air beneath his heels. He leaned as far back as he could, taking his weight on his arms. Feeding the rope hand over hand, he bounced steadily downwards.

When he glanced up he saw a trio of silhouettes watching him from the clifftop, about ten yards away. The moon, a bright semicircle, lit them from behind with an eerie halo. Each beast had three savage horns twisting from its skull and a wide, flat face. On their snouts, a single round nostril pumped steam into the air. Pedro had never seen anything so hideous, and his terror made him descend faster . . . until he felt the rope jerk violently.

He looked up and saw that one of the monsters had the rope in its mouth. It was thrashing its head angrily from side to side like a dog wrestling a bone. He felt a sudden tug on the rope, then another. Now the beast was hauling him up on the rope like a fish on the end of a line!

'Oww!' he shouted as his toes scraped up the cliff. He had only one option. Closing his eyes, he let go of the rope. His arms windmilled at his sides as he dropped. He hit the ground and grunted, crumpling into a heap on the soft purple sand.

If he could make it to his rowing boat, just a few yards away, he would be back on his ship within the hour. He stood up slowly. His ankle was twisted, but he didn't think he'd broken any bones. Surely he was safe now. But a sudden noise prompted him to look up – and his relief turned to pure panic.

The thick-shouldered, heavy-footed, cumbersome monsters were coming after him down the craggy cliff, moving on all fours as easily as a spider might scuttle down a wall. Pedro watched, frozen in horror, as they scurried down to the beach, their thick tails seeming to steady them on the sheer rock. Within seconds they had surrounded him.

'There, there,' he coaxed. 'Ni-i-i-ce monsters.'

One of them thrashed its tail against the small rowing boat on the beach. The boat crashed into the rocks as if it was a balsa-wood model, splintering into a pile of driftwood. The monsters screeched. Pedro retched at the awful stench of rotten eggs suddenly in his nostrils. One beast raised itself up on to two legs and walked towards him. Now its shape was more human than animal: a terrifying, grotesque ogre beating its clawed fists against its horned head.

Pedro knew he was doomed, but when he looked to the sky to whisper a final prayer he saw something that gave him a sliver of hope. Standing at the top of the cliff was a bulky figure whose fur coat shimmered in the moonlight.

'Hey, Erebus!' called Pedro frantically. 'Help me. Please.'

'You betrayed me,' the figure growled. 'Why should I help you now?'

'Because I'll tell you where it is,' said Pedro. 'I hid it on the island, but I have written down its location. If you save me I'll take you there.' He pulled the narrow piece of wood from his tunic and waved it at Prince Erebus. 'It's all on here, I promise.'

The beasts edged closer to Pedro as he cowered on the sand and, for a moment, the prince did nothing. Then he let out an almighty screech – the same noise the monsters had made earlier. In that moment the beasts stopped, and two of them loped angrily away and scaled the rock face as quickly as they had descended. They reached the top in seconds and circled the prince, their bellies flat on the ground like hunting lions. Erebus drew his sword. Its long steel blade flashed in the moonlight.

Both monsters leaped at the prince, who stepped back, then twisted and thrust his sword into the belly of one of them. There was a hideous squeal and the beast dropped to the ground. In one fluid motion the prince withdrew the blade and spun back, pirouetting towards the other creature. He swung the sword above his head and swiped it in a wide horizontal arc. This time there was no squeal.

5

The animal's body collapsed into a heap next to the prince. Its head, which had been sliced clean from its shoulders, tumbled down the cliff face, speeding up like a ball bouncing down some stairs. It landed on the beach with a thud, its single nostril still twitching sickeningly.

All together the animals on the beach let out a hideous cry. Pedro felt every hair on his body prickle with fear.

'Great, now I'm definitely going to be tonight's special,' he muttered.

But they weren't interested in Pedro any more. Every single monster had turned away and started climbing the cliff face, driven by some animal instinct to attack the one who had threatened their pack.

Pedro saw his chance to escape. His rowing boat was useless, but he was a strong swimmer. As he waded into the water he could hear the death squeals as another monster was slain. He knew the prince had no chance of killing all the creatures single-handedly, but he didn't care. All he was worried about was getting off the island alive. He was just about to plunge head first into the safety of the still, black water when something grabbed his shoulders.

'I can't bear it!' groaned Pedro. 'What now?'

He felt himself being yanked out of the water and up, up, up into the sky. He was flying! He was in the grip of some kind of huge bird with wings as big as the sails of a small boat. As he struggled, the small piece of wood fell from inside his tunic and tumbled silently away from his grasping hands.

Swiftly, Pedro was carried up over the cliff. He could see the prince below, surrounded by the monsters. For a moment he felt strangely secure, flying high above the deadly battle . . . then he realized that the bird was taking him down. Pedro kicked his legs defiantly as the bird swooped low over the pack of monsters. Just when he could make out the thick wiry hair on the beasts' backs he felt the bird release him, right into the middle of the pack.

The prince was swinging his steel blade just yards away. Pedro tried to scramble to his feet, but one of the monsters was now standing over him on its stocky hind legs. Its breath was putrid and its eyes were milky pink. It opened its mouth to reveal teeth as sharp as broken glass. A dollop of gooey saliva dripped on to Pedro, coating him in slime. The beast's mouth opened wider and wider.

'I must warn you I'm not very tasty,' simpered Pedro. 'I've hardly got any meat on my bones.'

The beast snorted and lunged. Its jaws snapped closed.

Chapter 1

Rupert Lilywhite handed his cloak to the young servant girl. He took off his hat and tossed back his long hair. The girl bobbed once and bustled away. Rupert strode to the drawing room, where his mother was embroidering a lace handkerchief.

'Pleasant walk, Rupert?' asked Lady Lilywhite.

'It's absolute bedlam in town,' said Rupert. 'There are commoners *everywhere*.'

'I suppose that's why they're called commoners.' Lady Lilywhite smiled. 'If they weren't everywhere they'd be un-commoners, wouldn't they?'

Rupert dabbed at his face with a powder puff. 'There was quite a commotion down at the docks,' he said wearily. 'Everyone was talking about some fellow called Columbus.'

'I know.' Lady Lilywhite beamed. 'Isn't it exciting?'

'Isn't what exciting? Who on earth *is* this Columbus chap?'

'He's the finest sailor the world has ever known,' said Lady Lilywhite. 'He's just returned from his great voyage.'

'But why is everyone making such a fuss over one dreary sailor?' Rupert sighed.

'Oh, he's not just any old sailor,' said Lady Lilywhite. 'He is admiral of the Spanish fleet, and he's an explorer. They say he sailed west across the Ocean Sea and discovered new land.'

'Whoopee,' said Rupert sarcastically.

'Apparently he's been granted an audience with Queen Isabella of Spain. He's going to present her with a fortune in treasure from his latest adventure.'

'Treasure?' said Rupert, suddenly perking up.

'In return the queen is going to make him a don.'

'A what?'

'I think it's like a Spanish nobleman,' said Lady Lilywhite. 'They say he'll soon be famous all over the world.'

'Just for sailing a boat across some water?'

'I know,' said Lady Lilywhite. 'In my day kings and queens were happy with invading their neighbours. These days they all want to take over a brand-new continent altogether. King Henry has offered a knighthood, and Cornwall, to any Englishman who can discover a new land.'

Rupert was in a trance. 'Sir Rupert Lilywhite of Cornwall,' he mumbled to himself. 'World-Famous Explorer and Friend of the King of England.'

*

Minutes later, Rupert threw open the door of his father's office.

'Father, we must talk,' he announced grandly.

Lord Lilywhite looked up from his desk. 'Are you all right, Rupert? You look like you've seen a ghost.'

'Yes, I'm fine,' Rupert snapped. 'I've just powdered my face, that's all. It's the height of fashion in France.'

Lord Lilywhite raised his eyebrows but said nothing.

'I have come to a decision about my future,' said Rupert. 'I am to sail the high seas.'

'Oh, that's marvellous,' said Lord Lilywhite. He had begun to worry that his son would never settle down to a career. 'I have some good friends in the navy. They will ensure you progress well.'

'The navy?' spat Rupert. 'I'm not going to join the navy. Do you take me for some sort of peasant? I want to be a famous explorer. You will buy me a ship so I can go and discover somewhere new.'

'I see.' Lord Lilywhite rubbed his eyes.

'I shall need a title too,' said Rupert. 'Just until the king gives me my knighthood.'

'Well, if you command your own ship, then you are the captain, I suppose.'

'Captain?' Rupert thought about this for a moment. 'I was thinking of something a little grander. I rather like the idea of being an admiral.'

And so, because Lord Lilywhite was a very wealthy

businessman, and because he thought Rupert was the best thing since salted pork, he commissioned a ship to be built for him. Lord Lilywhite also had many contacts in Europe. One of them happened to be a friend of Christopher Columbus, who knew the famous explorer was soon to visit England to recruit for his next voyage. He arranged for Rupert to meet Columbus to learn about discovering new lands.

But when Rupert met Columbus he didn't ask for any advice about sailing or navigating. Instead Rupert talked a lot about how rich and famous he would be once he had discovered a new continent. He also bragged about the ship that was being built for him.

'It's being constructed from solid oak,' said Rupert. 'Its main mast will be taller than any other ship's in the history of, er . . . very tall ships. And my cabin will be the most luxurious ever. It is to be upholstered in the finest buckskin leather.'

'Naturally,' said Christopher Columbus. (Although he was Italian he spoke many languages fluently.) 'And who will be your crew?'

'Crew?' said Rupert. 'Oh, I shall hire any old crew down at the docks – Father has given me plenty of money. But my ship will have the most divine figure-head.'

'I see.' Christopher Columbus stifled a yawn. 'What name will you choose for this vessel of yours?'

'Oh, nothing too grand – one doesn't want to blow one's own bugle.' A smile of satisfaction tickled Rupert's lips. 'I shall probably call it something terribly understated like the *Magnificent and Intrepid Rupert Lilywhite*.'

'How very, er, modest,' said Columbus. 'May I make a suggestion?'

'If you must,' said Rupert.

'I think a foreign name would signify your immense knowledge of the world and your spirit of adventure.'

Rupert nodded thoughtfully.

'There is a Spanish phrase that describes you perfectly,' said Christopher Columbus. 'You should call your ship *El Tonto Perdido*.'

Rupert thought the name sounded very glamorous indeed.

CHapter 2

Hugo Bailey and his uncle Walter left Daisy's Dockside Teashop holding their full bellies. They were celebrating Hugo's birthday and had just polished off two roast ferrets and a whole jam sponge between them.

'That was the best lunch ever,' said Hugo. 'Thank you, Uncle Walter.'

'Well, it isn't every day my favourite nephew turns twelve.' Walter pulled on a flat cloth cap. He had bushy white eyebrows and a thick moustache that covered his mouth. When he smiled – as he did then – his moustache twitched and the corners of his eyes crinkled. He put an arm round Hugo's shoulders and they set off along the cobbles.

Soon they came upon a small gathering of people on the quayside in front of a splendid ship. Hugo grabbed his uncle's sleeve. A very pale-looking man was preparing to address the crowd from the ship's helm.

Rupert Lilywhite had organized a public ceremony to christen *El Tonto Perdido*, which was undeniably a truly magnificent vessel. It had three huge masts, the tallest of which reached over two hundred feet into the sky. Its sails snapped eagerly in the wind, and above each sail rippled a purple silk flag bearing the initials R.L. in curly gold script.

The ship had raised decks at the front and rear and its crowning glory was the figurehead, handcrafted from oak and jutting proudly from the front of the ship. It was a carving of a man brandishing a sword in a gesture of leadership, his hair flowing behind him like a mane. He was grinning, as if laughing in the face of danger, and his hat was adorned with a cascade of feathers. It was a carving of someone Rupert Lilywhite thought would inspire awe in all who saw the ship. It was a carving of Rupert Lilywhite.

'Friends and admirers,' he began, 'as you all know I am the famous explorer Admiral Rupert Lilywhite . . .'

Rupert paused, expecting a round of applause, but nobody clapped. Most of the people there had never heard of him. They had only come along because the invitation to the ceremony had promised them a free drink and some roasted pig.

Someone in the crowd shouted, 'Where have you been exploring then?'

Rupert pretended not to hear. He continued, 'So, without further ado, I do hereby name this vessel *El Tonto Perdido*. May God have mercy on her and all who sail in her.'

There was a general murmur of confusion as the people in the crowd muttered under their breath.

'That's a strange name,' said one.

'It sounds foreign,' said another.

'It's Spanish,' said Uncle Walter. 'It means the *Lost Fool.*'

'Do you think he'll be recruiting for a voyage?' whispered Hugo.

Walter looked down at Hugo. His nephew beamed up at him with a gap-toothed smile. His round face was peppered with freckles and his excited blue eyes shone under a mop of curly blond hair. Walter knew exactly what Hugo was thinking, and he felt his heart sink.

Walter Bailey was a skilled mapmaker who had travelled all over the world, recording the progress of some of the great explorers. But his life had changed four years previously when he had been asked to join a voyage led by Bartolomeu Dias, who was attempting to be the first European ever to sail round the southernmost tip of Africa. At the time, Walter's younger brother, Jack, was a carpenter in a small village just outside Plymouth. Business was slow and he was falling behind with his rent. He was barely making enough money to feed his wife and his son, Hugo, and his landlord was threatening him with eviction. When he heard that Bartolomeu Dias was putting together a crew for his expedition, Jack wanted to join up alongside Walter.

Such expeditions were fraught with danger and he knew he would miss his family terribly, but the rewards were handsome. The money Jack would earn in six months at sea would be enough to pay off his debts and feed his family for years.

Walter tried to discourage Jack – he knew more than anyone that life at sea could be tough and dangerous – but his brother had made up his mind. So Walter spoke to Bartolomeu Dias, admitting that Jack had little experience as a sailor but pointing out that as a skilled carpenter he would be able to repair any damage the ships might encounter during the arduous voyage. Dias trusted Walter's judgement and hired Jack.

The night before setting off, Jack gave eight-year-old Hugo a wooden chess piece that he had carved into the shape of a horse's head. Chess was Hugo's favourite game and the knight was his favourite piece because it could always manoeuvre itself out of trouble. The edge of the base was engraved with the words 'Honest, Undaunted, Gallant, Optimistic.'

'What does it mean?' asked Hugo.

'Well, what do the initials spell?' said his father.

Hugo studied his piece for a moment. 'Hugo!' he said with a smile.

'Exactly!' His father smiled back. 'These are the qualities that make you who you are.'

*

From that day on Hugo wore the wooden knight on a string round his neck and spent hour upon hour studying it, even though at first he didn't entirely understand the full meaning of the words. He would turn the knight over in his hands when he was nervous and clutch it to his chest in his sleep.

Bartolomeu Dias took two ships on his voyage. As Dias's mapmaker, Walter sailed aboard the lead ship, while Jack was assigned to the support vessel. Within months they had navigated the treacherous southern oceans and succeeded in rounding the tip of Africa, which Dias named the Cape of Storms.

Soon after the expedition had turned for home it encountered a horrendous storm – the worst that any of the sailors had ever experienced. The ferocious sea tossed the ships about like leaves in the wind. Huge waves dwarfed the boats before engulfing them in foam and brine. The sailors huddled below deck and prayed for the sea gods to have mercy on them.

After many days the storm passed and Walter went up on deck with Dias. The horizon to the north was calm – a single undisturbed line. Then, as he surveyed the horizon to the south, east and west, a horrible realization wrapped around Walter like a cold cloak. Desperately he studied the ocean as the panic gripped his throat tighter and tighter. But he saw nothing – and his worst fears were confirmed. The second boat was missing.

After days of searching they eventually had to accept the evidence. Jack's ship was lost – presumed sunk.

When Walter returned home he went straight to Jack's wife to pass on the terrible news. But there was another family living in their home, and Walter learned that Alice had been taken ill soon after her husband had gone to sea. The doctors had done all they could, even covering her with leeches to suck out the evil disease, but it had been no use. Hugo's mother had passed away.

Walter found a tired, scrawny and miserable Hugo at the workhouse for orphaned children. He had a red welt on the palm of his hand from clutching his wooden pendant tightly every night. When the master of the workhouse saw just how keen Walter was to take away his nephew, he became very reluctant to let go of 'the poor precious boy'. It was not until Walter offered him a huge sum of money – most of his savings, in fact – that the master relented. ('Anything for the precious boy's happiness, of course.')

And so Hugo came to live with his uncle Walter. Walter gave up travelling, despite the fact that enticing job offers continued to come his way. Even when

Christopher Columbus himself asked him to join the crew of the *Santa Maria*, he turned down the offer.

To begin with, Walter had missed his life as a map-maker and the great satisfaction he earned from adding fresh detail to the evolving world map. But life at sea was too dangerous for a boy of Hugo's age, and Walter had vowed to take care of his brother's son. Whenever his nephew asked him about his adventures he would change the subject. Walter was determined not to encourage any curiosity Hugo might have had about the world beyond England's shores so he gathered up all his maps and charts and locked them away in his study with his mapmaking instruments.

Since then Walter had tried to make ends meet by selling street maps of the city, but business was slow. No one needed a map to find their way around. There was only one main street so it was almost impossible to get lost.

With no steady income and no prospect of regular employment Walter had to pay the rent and feed Hugo from what little savings he had left. Treats were scarce, but Walter and Hugo were happy. Walter helped Hugo with his schoolwork, and Hugo taught Walter how to play chess. From time to time Hugo pleaded with his uncle to take him away on a voyage somewhere.

'You know what I think about exploring,' Walter

would say, his kind eyes twinkling. 'It's far too dangerous.'

As soon as the free food ran out the crowd dispersed
from in front of *El Tonto Perdido*, but Hugo remained
standing on the dockside, staring up at the ship.

'Why don't we ask if he needs a mapmaker for his
voyage?' asked Hugo. 'Now that I'm twelve I don't have
to go to school any more. I could be your apprentice.'

Walter laughed nervously. 'You'd be far better off
taking up an apprenticeship with a draughtsman or a
shipbuilder,' he said, ushering Hugo homewards.
'Besides, you don't know the first thing about mapmaking!'

Hugo took one last look at the ship. He wondered if
it would soon be time to let Uncle Walter know the
truth.

Chapter 3

On the way home, they passed pie sellers shouting about their produce in booming voices and children chasing each other and playing hopscotch on chalk grids. A crowd had gathered to watch actors performing a play in the street while others cheered a man juggling wooden balls. Outside the guildhall two men were clamped into the stocks by their wrists. Passers-by stopped to jeer and pelt them with rotten vegetables, and Hugo wondered what crime the men could have committed to deserve their punishment.

Eventually they turned off the main street into the narrow and gloomy Peppercorn Alley. Walter opened the front door and waved Hugo into the tiny house.

'Home sweet home, my boy!'

The small building had a simple wooden frame and a floor of dry mud. A trestle table with two benches almost filled the living room. There were two small bedrooms, a study that was kept locked and a single narrow window with a scenic view of the open sewer flowing past their door.

Walter knelt by the fireplace and arranged some sticks in the grate. He banged two stones together to make a spark and soon a small fire lit the room. He placed a turnip and a few carrots on the table and began to cut them up.

'And how would sir like his vegetables cooked this evening?' asked Walter.

'Boiled as usual, please,' said Hugo with a smile.

'Certainly, sir.' Walter tried to smile back, but he was ashamed of how they had to live. At least on board a ship Hugo would be fed regularly. And the boy would get to see the world, not just the gutter. But Walter sighed – he refused to be responsible for another relative being lost at sea.

That night Hugo awoke soon after midnight. He tiptoed past Walter's bedroom and stepped round the trestle table. The room was dark, but Hugo had done this so often he could have managed with his eyes shut. He silently retrieved a large clay pot from its shelf and placed it on the table. He took out a key and slid it into the locked study door, holding his breath as he turned it. The levers and hinges were well oiled and he opened the door without a sound. Hugo closed it behind him and lit a lantern.

For many months after going to live with his uncle, Hugo had wondered what lay behind the locked door. 'Nothing of concern to you,' was always Uncle Walter's reply.

Then, one day, Hugo had discovered the key by chance while searching for a missing chess piece. Curiosity had lured him through the locked door that very evening, and fascination had brought him back every night since.

Now his heart raced as he looked around. Scores of rolled-up parchments leaned against the rough walls and lay on flat wooden shelves. Eagerly he grabbed a tube and spread its contents on the small table, the paper crackling loudly as he smoothed it with his palms.

Hugo loved the smell of the maps – the aroma of ink and oil and dust. He loved the way each map would hint at history and secrets and the promise of adventure. Tracing the coastlines with his finger, he tried to picture the lands they enclosed. His finger wandered down the west coast of Africa, to the Cape of Storms. Then it ventured out to sea and meandered briefly in ever-decreasing circles.

Mesmerized, Hugo took his hand away and scanned the world with wide eyes. There were so many countries, each with its own distinct shape and size – its own unique character. It still amazed him just how small England was. The only land he had ever known was a tiny speck compared to the rest of the world. (And even *that* was only the land that had been discovered so far.) 'I wonder what else is out there?' muttered Hugo.

The names on the maps excited him too – Bohemia, Constantinople, Arabia, Mozambique. He had often listened to Uncle Walter telling his father about the deserts and mountains and oceans depicted on his charts, and he was hungry to experience for himself the colours and sounds and smells these exotic places could offer. Well, thought Hugo, maybe soon the feast would begin.

He was certainly ready for it. Mapmaking was a science as well as an art and Hugo had been studying hard. At night he would secretly examine Walter's maps and his extensive writings. He studied trigonometry and astronomy, he learned how to measure latitude using the stars or the sun, and how to estimate the speed of a boat on the open sea.

That night as he locked the door behind him and returned the key to the clay pot he felt satisfied but impatient. He had memorized all the mapmaking techniques described in Uncle Walter's texts. Now it was time to try them out for real.

Chapter 4

Admiral Rupert Lilywhite arrived at the dockside at noon. He planned to set sail the very next day and all the important arrangements had been made. The only thing that remained was the small matter of finding a crew to sail *El Tonto Perdido* while he was busy doing whatever it was that famous explorers did on their ships.

Rupert scanned the dockside for anyone he thought looked like a sailor. Soon a tattooed, stubbly-faced man with long straggly hair caught Rupert's eye because he seemed a bit unsteady on his feet. Even when he was standing still his whole body swayed like a sapling in a gale. Rupert had heard that very experienced sailors become so used to the motion of a boat that they have trouble standing up on dry land. The tattooed man was having so much trouble standing up that Rupert decided he must be a *very* experienced sailor indeed.

'Ahoy there, me hearty,' said Rupert, trying his best to use the correct sailors' lingo. 'I'm looking to hire a crew to sail my ship.' He gestured grandly at *El Tonto Perdido*.

The tattooed man wobbled, looked at the ship, wobbled again and peered back at Rupert, squeezing one eye closed in an effort to focus. 'Eh?' he said.

Rupert continued. 'I intend to pay handsomely for an experienced sailor who commands an expert crew of seamen.'

To illustrate his claim Rupert took out a purse full of gold coins and hefted it in his hand as if he was guessing its weight.

The wobbly tattooed man peered at the purse. 'In that case, I am indeed a handsome sailor with an experienced crew and I am willing to be paid expertly,' he mumbled.

'What is the furthest you have sailed to?' said Rupert.

'On our last voyage, we been all the way to Land's End and back,' said the wobbly tattooed sailor.

Rupert had never heard of Land's End, but thought it sounded like somewhere very exciting on the other side of the world. (It was actually only a few miles along the southern coast of England.) So he hired the sailor and arranged to meet him and his crew on board *El Tonto Perdido* the next morning.

'By the way, matey,' said Rupert, 'I didn't catch your name.'

The sailor removed his hat and clutched it to his chest.

'I'm terribly sorry, sir,' he said, bowing unsteadily. 'I'm Oliver Muddle.'

*

From a distance Hugo watched the two men who were deep in conversation. That morning he had told Uncle Walter he had a tummy ache, probably from eating too much roast ferret the day before. Walter had left Hugo in bed and gone to the town square to try to sell some maps. Hugo had waited about ten minutes before dressing and hurrying to the dockside.

He had recognized Admiral Lilywhite as soon as he'd arrived at the quay. The admiral was dressed in a scarlet doublet and hose, with cream stockings and a thick cream feather in his three-cornered hat. His long brown hair was tied back with a black velvet bow and his face was as white as a circus clown's. He had a neat little moustache that contrasted with his soapy skin.

The other man was big and hairy and quite obviously drunk.

Curious to hear what they were talking about, Hugo wandered innocently past.

'I want all of your crew to report on deck at seven o'clock tomorrow,' the admiral was saying.

'What, in the *morning*?' said the drunk.

'Yes, of course,' said the admiral. 'We set sail at nine o'clock sharp.'

Hugo's heart was racing. They would be sailing tomorrow! He stopped a few yards past the men and waited until they had finished their conversation. He watched the sailor weave his way along the quayside before approaching Admiral Lilywhite.

'Good day, sir,' said Hugo, bowing his head politely. 'Are you crewing for an imminent voyage, by any chance?'

'My ship is fully crewed,' replied Rupert, barging past.

Hugo watched Rupert walk away for a moment, then he called after him, 'May I enquire who your map-maker is, sir?'

Rupert stopped and turned back. 'Mapmaker?'

'Yes, sir,' said Hugo.

'I don't have a mapmaker.'

'Then how will you show everyone back in England all the places you have discovered?'

'I . . . I . . . I hadn't thought of that,' said Rupert. 'I suppose I'll have to do it myself.'

Hugo smiled winningly. 'Sir, everyone knows that Columbus has his own mapmaker. He's far too busy dis-covering continents to be bothered with drawing maps. As a famous explorer yourself, wouldn't you agree that you also are much too important to chart your own progress?'

'Yes,' said Rupert, smirking proudly, 'I suppose I am, aren't I?'

'I have studied for years under the great Walter Bailey – mapmaker to Bartolomeu Dias himself.'

Rupert had never heard of Bartolomeu Dias, but he guessed he was probably famous from the way the boy said his name. 'In that case, you're hired,' Rupert said. 'As you probably know, I am Admiral Rupert Lilywhite. You may call me Admiral. And you are?'

'My name is Hugo Bailey.'

Hugo watched Admiral Lilywhite walk away. Then he gazed up at the imposing ship with purple silk flags and imagined it sailing across the Ocean Sea. Now his tummy really was churning.

Hugo was back in bed when Walter came home late that evening.

'Sell any maps?' Hugo asked.

Walter shook his head. 'Are you feeling better?' he said, kneeling next to Hugo.

'Not really,' said Hugo. 'I think I'm just going to try to sleep.'

'Poor boy,' said Walter, giving Hugo a hug. 'Sleep tight.'

Hugo put his arms round Walter's neck and grabbed two fistfuls of his uncle's shirt. 'Thank you, Uncle Walter.'

'What for?' said Walter, looking startled.

'For looking after me. I mean, er, when I'm ill and everything.'

Walter smiled and ruffled his nephew's blond curls. 'You're a good boy, Hugo,' he said as he left the room.

Hugo was up before sunrise. Silently he unlocked the study and took a long wooden box down from the top shelf. He unlatched the lid and carefully lifted out Uncle Walter's backstaff, wiping it with a soft cloth. It was made of two wooden battens fixed together to make a V-shape, two curved scales, a small vane and a sight. Barely breathing, he placed the backstaff back in its box, and put the box into his leather satchel. Next, he set out some parchment, quills and ink, a measuring rope, some sea charts and a mariner's compass. He packed them all along with a notebook and some charcoal and pulled on his tunic.

He paused outside Uncle Walter's bedroom. He felt so guilty about deserting him that, for a moment, he considered staying. But he would be back within the year. By then he too would be an experienced explorer, and he would know more about the ocean that had claimed his father. Hugo gripped his pendant and recited its inscription to himself.

Honest, Undaunted, Gallant, Optimistic.

It was time to prove that he was worthy of his father's belief in him and show Uncle Walter how much he had learned. It was time to make them both proud.

'See you in six months, Uncle Walter,' he whispered.

CHapter 5

Hugo reported to *El Tonto Perdido* at seven o'clock sharp. Admiral Rupert Lilywhite showed him to the cabin, which was a gloomy room below the raised deck at the front of the ship. It had no windows and no furniture. Hugo guessed that musty blankets piled up in the corner were intended as the crew's beds. In a shadowy corner he could just make out another figure kneeling by a blanket.

'How many sailors will sleep in here?' he asked.

'About fifteen at a time,' said Rupert, smiling. 'It'll be lovely and cosy for you all.'

'That's fine,' said Hugo. 'I don't take up much room anyway.'

'Naturally you'll be working alongside my chief mapmaker. So you'd better get used to each other.'

'Er . . . sorry?' said Hugo. 'I thought I was your mapmaker.'

'This chap collared me at the docks yesterday – just after I spoke to you, in fact,' said Rupert. 'He's obviously very experienced. He says he's worked with . . . now who was it again?' Rupert frowned. 'Well, his name escapes me but he was some foreign chap who had explored somewhere or other. Anyway, he persuaded me to take him on so your job description has been adjusted ever so slightly.'

'You mean I've been demoted?' said Hugo.

'"Demoted" is such an *ugly* word,' said Rupert smarmily. 'Let's just say you've been outranked.'

Hugo didn't like the sound of this. 'That's not fair,' he muttered, wishing he could think of something more grown-up to say.

The figure in the corner had stood up and was now approaching. 'Nobody said life at sea was fair,' said Rupert.

'But I'm not a child and I don't need a babysitter,' said Hugo, trying to keep his voice as deep as possible. 'I know all there is to know about mapmaking. I don't need somebody to tell me how to do my job.'

'Don't worry.' The mysterious figure now spoke. 'Let's just say that I'm the mapmaker and you are my apprentice.' As he spoke he stepped forward and the light from Rupert's lantern fell across his face.

Hugo couldn't believe his eyes. 'Uncle Walter?' he cried.

'Oh good, you two know each other,' said Rupert. 'That makes this whole thing *so* much less awkward. Well, I'll leave you to it.'

Hugo and Uncle Walter smiled at one another as the admiral struggled up the ladder to the main deck.

'I thought you were asleep at home,' said Hugo sheepishly.

Uncle Walter's moustache twitched. 'It's amazing what people get up to when they're supposed to be in bed, isn't it?' he said.

'Whatever do you mean?' said Hugo as innocently as he could.

'Well, my boy, I've known about your midnight studies for a long time.'

'But I was always so careful not to make any noise.'

'Precisely. I haven't oiled that lock or those hinges for years, but they still don't make a squeak. I guessed someone had been oiling them for a reason.' Walter's voice was quiet and warm. 'I saw your expression when you laid eyes on this ship. I knew I couldn't keep you at home for much longer.'

'I'm sorry I didn't tell you I was leaving. But why didn't you stop me?'

Uncle Walter shrugged. 'I wanted to see how determined you are. I would never encourage you to explore, but I can't stand in your way either.'

Hugo gave his uncle a grateful smile. He had finally proved that he had the nerve to join an expedition on his own – but he was actually rather relieved that Uncle Walter was going with him. It was one thing to read about mapmaking in his uncle's study, but it would be quite another to put it into practice on the open seas, hundreds of miles from home.

'I wonder where our voyage will take us,' said Hugo dreamily.

'I wonder.' Walter nodded. 'Admiral Lilywhite didn't go into any details about his plan. That's if he's got one at all.'

'I hope we go somewhere tropical,' said Hugo. 'Maybe a jungle, or a volcanic island. We'll catch fish for our supper and drink coconut milk. We might trek for days through the jungle and climb to the very rim of the volcano's crater. There might be natives in the jungle as well. They'll be scared of us because of our pale skin and they'll probably try to capture us! But when we explain that we are friends they'll invite us to their homes – wooden huts built high up in the trees. They'll give us spears and shields and ask us to defend them from rival tribes.'

'Slow down, Hugo.' Walter laughed. 'We haven't even set sail yet and you're already befriending the natives. You have to be patient. Days at sea are long, and it may be weeks before we find land. But first we have work to do. We must check all our equipment.'

Walter and Hugo unpacked and went back up on deck. Oliver Muddle and his crew had finally arrived. There were about thirty sailors loading supplies for the voyage, all looking like they needed a bath and a shave, followed by a long sleep. Their clothes were stained and grimy and together they gave off a nasty aroma of stale ale and old sweat. As well as boxes of food, they were loading a colossal mountain of beer barrels and a large wooden cage in which a dozen hens strutted up and down.

Rupert was trying to make a speech about the impending voyage, but nobody was listening. The sailors were already passing tankards round and filling them with beer. Rupert couldn't help noticing that they were all swaying unsteadily: even *he* knew that sailors were only supposed to have trouble standing up when they were on dry land. He wondered if there was another reason for their wobbly legs.

'Seaman Muddle,' called Rupert, realization suddenly dawning, 'do you think it's right that the crew should be standing around drinking ale?'

Oliver Muddle looked thoughtful for a moment. 'Absolutely not, Admiral, sir,' he said. He turned to the sailors. 'Listen, men. The admiral doesn't want you standing around drinking, and I think he's right. So why don't you all sit down and relax.'

'Let's hear it for the admiral,' shouted one of the sailors. All the men cheered and slumped on to the deck.

This wasn't quite what Rupert had in mind, but he

was rather pleased to be such a hit with his crew so he let the matter drop.

'By the way, Seaman Muddle,' he said, 'what is the purpose of the hens?'

'Eggs,' said Oliver Muddle with a smile. 'The men love their eggs in the morning. It's where they get all their energy from.'

'Well, I wouldn't want a lazy crew, would I?' said Rupert. 'I'll allow them one drink now, but I want them all presented for briefing in two orderly lines in ten minutes.'

An hour later, the sailors tottered on the main deck in a shambolic huddle. Walter and Hugo stood smartly at the starboard side of the deck. Rupert appeared on the raised deck at the ship's stern and surveyed his crew. His face was freshly powdered and his hat was adorned with a most elaborate arrangement of colourful feathers.

'Is that a parrot on his head?' whispered one of the sailors, causing the others to snigger furiously.

Rupert puffed out his chest and smoothed down his thin moustache with the knuckle of his forefinger.

'Men!' he said. 'As your admiral I would like to share with you my vision for our expedition. We will set sail in one hour. We will steer a westerly course and . . .' Rupert realized he had reached the end of his plan. He struggled for something else to say. '. . . and we will discover a whole new continent. Or a brand-new country, or an island or something.'

As the crew shuffled away, Rupert wished he'd rehearsed his speech a little more.

The ship sailed at two o'clock in the afternoon. Oliver Muddle steered while the crew hauled on ropes and raised the sails. Rupert posed on the prow of the ship, peering through his telescope as though he was looking for something very important. Soon, though, his arms got too tired to continue holding up the telescope. Instead he just stood with his hands on his hips and tried to look purposeful, occasionally stroking his moustache.

Walter and Hugo stood together on the high deck at the stern of the ship, watching England slowly recede into the distance. When he couldn't see the coastline any more Hugo felt another wave of anxiety sweep over him.

Walter put a hand on his shoulder and squeezed gently. 'Don't worry, Hugo,' he said. 'Home will be waiting for us when we get back. Now, let's go and prepare the charts.'

They returned to the cabin, where they spread a huge map across the oak floor. On the far right of the sheet was drawn the westernmost coastline of Europe. The rest of the page was blank, except for a very faint grid of large squares.

'Do you think there's land out there, Uncle Walter?' asked Hugo, carefully laying out a divider.

'We'll just have to wait and see,' said Walter. 'But we must keep our wits about us. I suspect the crew will need our help if we're going to navigate across the ocean!'

Later, when Walter and Hugo went back on deck, they found Rupert strutting up and down the rear deck.

'Has there been a change of plan, Admiral?' said Walter.

'No, indeed,' said Rupert. 'The planned plan was planned with proper planning. I see no reason to alter the plan.'

'I see,' said Walter tactfully.

'Why are we going south, then?' asked Hugo, less tactfully. 'You said the plan was to sail west.'

'Don't be ridiculous, boy!' snapped Rupert. 'What makes you think we're going south?'

'Well,' said Hugo, 'the sun is setting over there.' He pointed over the starboard side of the ship, where orange sunlight was bleeding through the evening clouds.

'I can see that.'

'And if the sun is setting off to our right then we can't be going west.'

'What are you twittering about?'

'Well, everybody knows that the sun sets in the west,' said Hugo.

Rupert frowned. 'Does it?' he said, looking to Walter for confirmation.

'Yes, Admiral,' said Walter. 'The sun rises in the east and sets in the west.'

'What, *every* day?' said Rupert.

Hugo and Walter nodded together. 'Every day.'

'Turn hard to starboard, Seaman Muddle!' screamed Rupert, his face purple with rage. 'We should be sailing into the sun, you twit. Everybody knows the sun sets in the west – every day.'

Chapter 6

El Tonto Perdido sailed for weeks on end. The crew worked in two shifts. They were on duty for four hours, then they rested for four hours, day and night. Hugo helped out with swabbing the decks and mending sails. It was his job to look after the ship's sandglass. As soon as the sand had run out he had to turn the glass over and shout out the time of day.

Every day at noon Hugo and Walter measured the angle of the sun with the backstaff. The sun shone through the sight and cast the shadow of the vane on to the curved scales. By reading the two scales they could work out their latitude. Walter estimated the ship's average speed to calculate their longitude. By plotting their position on the chart they could check that the boat was sailing a westerly course. Very roughly, it was.

The sailors fascinated Hugo. He often spied on them when he wasn't helping Walter. When they weren't hoisting sails or climbing the rigging they spent the days singing or playing cards. In the evening, those who weren't on watch passed the hours by gambling. They staged races with rats or cockroaches they'd caught, placing bets on which would be the first to scurry past the finish line. At supper they would tap their biscuits on the table before eating them. This shook loose any maggots that might have burrowed into the food, and then they competed to see who could swallow the most maggots in a minute.

They even placed bets on their admiral. They gambled on how long he would spend peering through his telescope at the empty horizon (usually around thirty minutes) or powdering his face and combing his hair (at least an hour and a half). One day, following a storm, the sailors wagered on how many times he would throw up over the side of the ship. (The correct guess was seventeen.)

Hugo also enjoyed listening to the sailors swapping tales of their expeditions. And what adventures they'd all had!

The one they called Swipe was small and wiry with straggly hair and crooked teeth. He had fought pirates in the Bay of Biscay, single-handedly killing eight of them in one battle alone by running them through with his cutlass.

Another sailor, Hawkeye, wore a patch over one eye, but said he had perfect sight in the other. He bragged about his twenty vision and spent the days in the crow's nest at the top of the main mast, looking for land. He told how he had wrestled sea tigers with his bare hands

in India, and fought off mountain dragons in the Pyre-
nees.

Rockford was as big as a shed and seemed to be made
of solid muscle. He claimed to have four parallel scars
that ran from his collarbone to his belly button, but he
wouldn't show them to anyone because they were too
hideous. According to Rockford, a giant razor-clawed
wolf had mauled his chest, but he had courageously
gone on to kill and eat it. Apparently it had tasted just
like chicken.

Excited by the tales he had heard, Hugo would
repeat them to his uncle in awed tones. Walter would
always raise an eyebrow and say, 'Gosh, they certainly
do tell some excellent stories.'

'OUCH!' yelped Hugo one morning.

He was on his hands and knees scrubbing the deck
under the blue sky and the hot sun. The wet brush had
slipped and he'd scraped his hand along the oak floor.
A shard of wood had gone into his finger.

'Splinter is it, my lad?' asked Oliver Muddle. 'You'd
better come with me to see the ship's doctor. Rusty will
fix you up.'

'I thought Rusty was the ship's cook,' said Hugo.

'He is.' Muddle grinned. 'He is a man of many tal-
ents – and many knives.'

*

In the galley, Rusty Cleaver grabbed Hugo's wrist and examined his finger. He nodded wisely to himself and pushed Hugo's hand on to the table.

'I can get rid of your splinter in a flash,' said Rusty. He wiped his free hand on his bloody apron and surveyed his tools. They consisted of a selection of implements – all of which had very large blades. The knife he chose was the one he'd just been using to cut up the pickled beef he was preparing for the sailors' dinner. Rusty gripped Hugo's wrist more tightly and raised the knife above his head.

'Wait,' said Hugo. 'You're not going to cut off my finger just for a splinter, are you?'

Rusty began to cackle. He looked at Oliver Muddle, who started to cackle too.

'Of course I'm not going to cut off your finger,' said Rusty. 'I'm going to cut off your whole hand. I can't be fiddling around all day cutting off individual fingers. I've got to bake a Henry sponge for the admiral's tea.'

'Don't worry, laddie,' said Oliver Muddle. 'We'll get you a nice shiny hook instead – once the bleeding has stopped.'

'But I want to keep my hand,' whimpered Hugo. 'I'm very attached to it.'

'Don't start snivelling,' sneered Muddle. 'It's not the end of the world.'

Hugo pulled his hand free and backed towards the door. 'It's only a splinter,' he said.

'If you don't have the operation, it could get infected,' said Rusty. 'Your finger might get gangrene and that could spread up your whole arm and into your brain. Your head will shrivel to the size of a fist and your eyes will fall out. You'll probably die a slow, horrible death, screaming for mercy.'

Hugo looked at Rusty Cleaver and Oliver Muddle.

'I'll think about it,' he said. He turned and hurried back up on deck.

The weather was changing. The sky was gloomy and a cool breeze swelled the ship's sails. The sea was all peaks and troughs like a rocky mountain range. Up ahead a black cloud stretched across the horizon and billowed up to the heavens.

Hugo watched the sailors lowering the sails with an air of urgency he hadn't sensed before. He found Uncle Walter up on the rear deck with Admiral Lilywhite.

'So what do you advise?' Rupert was saying.

'It's almost certainly just a storm,' said Walter. 'I recommend you maintain course and ride it out.'

'It does look frightfully black though,' said Rupert. 'Are you sure we won't just fall off the edge of the world?'

'Well, you *could* turn round,' said Walter. 'Of course

Christopher Columbus sailed further west than this, but if you're afraid . . .'

'Maintain course!' Rupert called down to Swipe, who was manning the tiller. The admiral's hands trembled as he raised his telescope once more.

Walter noticed that his nephew had come up on deck. 'Where have you been, Hugo?' he asked.

'Oh, Rusty wanted me to give him a hand in the galley, that's all. What's happening?'

'The men think we have reached the edge of the world,' said Walter. The ship pitched violently and he grabbed hold of his nephew. 'They believe the world is flat and that if we sail too far we will fall off the edge into oblivion.'

'Is that true?' asked Hugo. Heavy rain had begun to pelt on to the decks. A white flash lit up the sky for a second, followed by a crackle of thunder.

Walter smiled. 'Most scientists believe the world is a globe. I've certainly never seen the edge of the world in any of my previous voyages. The sailors' fears are probably unfounded.'

'*Probably?*' said Hugo.

'We don't know enough about the world to be absolutely sure,' said Walter. 'It's up to explorers like us to find the answers.'

Hugo nodded resolutely, but he was feeling a little

queasy – and not just because the ship was rocking and rolling.

Seaman Muddle climbed up to the rear deck, his eyes wild with fear. His soaking hair was plastered to his head and his shirt was stuck to his belly.

'Admiral!' he shouted through the storm. 'You must turn this ship round.'

'I'll do no such thing,' said Rupert. 'If Christopher Columbus can sail further than this, then so can I.'

'But we could all be killed,' said Oliver Muddle.

'It's probably just a thunderstorm,' said Walter.

'And what if you're wrong, old man?' Muddle was frantic. 'What if we all plunge to our deaths?'

'Don't panic, Seaman Muddle,' said Hugo, smiling. 'It's not the end of the world.'

It was a ferocious storm. The ship was lashed by pounding rain, and the angry seas tossed it about like a cork. Some of the sailors huddled together and prayed, others drank even more beer than usual and wailed that they were all about to die. Admiral Lilywhite hid in his cabin and was sick – a lot. The rain had washed the powder from his face, but his complexion was still deathly white.

Walter braced himself in a corner of the crew's cabin and held on to Hugo, who in turn pressed his head against his uncle's chest, clinging on to him for dear life. When the ship pitched up the face of the mountainous waves, it felt like it might tip on to its back. When it plunged down the other side Hugo imagined they might be swallowed whole by the ocean. Sea water crashed over the bows and drowned the ship's decks. Anything that wasn't secured was washed overboard.

Hugo wondered if it would ever end. But the sun came up the next day and, as quickly as it had started, the storm died away. The clouds cleared and the sea flattened.

At first the sailors were reluctant to go up on deck. Only when they were sure that the ship wasn't about to fall over the edge of the world did they return to their duties. Warily at first, they pumped the sea water from the ship, and mended the sails. They climbed the rigging and swabbed the decks. Slowly everything went back to normal.

Walter removed the splinter from Hugo's finger. He poured boiling water over one point of his dividers, then he used it to pick out the sliver of wood. Hugo's hand didn't develop gangrene. Neither did his head shrivel up, nor did his eyes fall out.

In the evenings, Hugo and Walter played chess or they went up on deck to study the stars. Now that the sky was clear again, Walter taught Hugo how to recognize some of the constellations.

'Over there is the Plough,' said Walter one night, pointing to the twinkling sky. He pressed his head against Hugo's so they could both look along his outstretched finger as he traced the shape of a plough.

'I see it!' cried Hugo.

'It's also known as the Great Bear.'

'How can it be a plough and a bear?' said Hugo.

'You just have to look at it another way,' explained Walter. He traced the stars together in a different order.

Hugo was amazed. 'I can see the bear too!'

'As a mapmaker you must always remember that there's more than one way of looking at things,' said Walter.

Hugo thought about this for a moment and nodded earnestly.

'I love studying the sky when it's this clear,' said Walter. 'I feel like I can see forever.'

Hugo smiled. 'I know,' he said. 'It's hard to imagine it could ever be cloudy again.'

But while he was relieved that they'd survived the storm, the monotony of life on the ship had started to frustrate him. Hours turned to days, days turned to weeks and weeks became months. Hugo started to feel like there was nothing else in the whole ocean but that little ship and the sailors it carried.

Then, one day, the ship hit something solid.

Chapter 7

A loud thump echoed through the cabins below decks. The ship lurched, throwing some of the sailors to the floor.

'Have we found dry land at last?' gasped Hugo.

'I'm not sure,' said Walter. 'Let's go and see.'

They hurried up to the deck. The sailors were already gathered along the starboard bow, scrutinizing the water below.

Hugo and Walter joined the huddle. There was no land in sight; the sea was flat and never-ending, the water deep and turquoise.

'Seaman Swipe,' called Admiral Lilywhite, emerging from his cabin, 'what have we hit?'

Swipe shrugged. 'Ain't nothing there, Admiral.'

'There must be *something* there, you twit.'

Just then there was another thump – this time on the opposite bow – and the ship lurched again. Everyone scurried across to peer over the other side. Again there was nothing to see but flat sea and deep water.

'Maybe it's a ghost,' said Rockford. His voice was strangely high for such a big man.

Hugo was sure the other sailors were going to laugh at this ridiculous idea.

'Aye, that'll be it,' said Oliver Muddle. ''Tis the, er, Demon of the Deep.'

Hugo was sure Seaman Muddle had just made this name up, but the other sailors nodded knowingly.

'The Demon of the Deep was what sunk two of da Gama's ships in the Mediterranean,' said Hawkeye.

'Yeah,' agreed Swipe. 'It swallows ships whole.'

'I seen it once,' claimed Rusty Cleaver. 'It's got jaws as wide as this boat. And tentacles twice as long.'

Hugo looked up at Uncle Walter. He smiled at his nephew and shook his head.

'Look over there!' someone yelled. 'There it is!'

About thirty yards off the starboard bow, some kind of giant fish leaped out of the water. It traced a perfect arc and plunged back into the ocean. Everyone gasped.

'Man the harpoons!' shouted Oliver Muddle. 'The Demon of the Deep is nigh.'

The creature leaped out of the water again. This time it was close enough for Hugo to get a good look. It was about twelve yards long; its body was round at the front and tapered like a teardrop. It had a flat fishtail and a single curved fin on its back. But it also had four big flippers that it used to push itself through the water. Seawater sprayed out of a hole in the top of its head and its nose was long, with a rounded end.

The creature dived under the boat. There was

another thump before it leaped out of the water on the opposite side.

'Kill the Demon!' ordered Oliver Muddle. 'It's trying to sink us.'

'Wait,' cried Hugo. 'That's not a demon.'

'That's the Demon, all right,' said Rusty.

'You said it had long tentacles and jaws as wide as this boat.'

Rusty hesitated.

'It did, last time I saw it,' he said, playing for time. 'But it . . . it can change its shape, you see.'

'That's right,' the other sailors agreed in unison. 'It's one of them shape-shifters.' They shuddered and went back to the business of getting the harpoons ready.

'It's not a demon,' Walter insisted. 'It's just a porpoisaur – one of the gentlest mammals in the ocean. There must only be a handful still alive in the world. If you kill this one, they'll be one step closer to extinction. Besides, it's not trying to sink us – it's playing with us. It thinks our boat is another fish.'

The sailors ignored him. Rockford picked up a harpoon and held it above his head like a spear. Hugo knew he had to act quickly. Seeing a knife that Rusty had left lying on the deck, he grabbed it and chopped at part of the rigging. The sail it had been holding dropped to the deck and landed on top of Rockford, swamping him under an ocean of canvas.

The sailor cursed as he fought his way out from under the sail, scowling at Hugo. He picked up another harpoon and waited for his target to come closer.

'We have to do something,' Hugo said to his uncle. 'We can't let them kill that poor porpoisaur.'

'There's nothing we can do,' said Walter sadly. 'There's nothing these sailors believe in more strongly than superstitions. Their whole existence is governed by tales of angels and demons.'

'Angels and demons, eh?' asked Hugo, an idea forming. He walked over and stood next to Oliver Muddle. Together they watched the porpoisaur frolicking in the ocean.

'It's funny,' remarked Hugo.

'What's funny?' said Seaman Muddle.

'Oh, nothing really. I was just thinking.'

There was another thump and the boat lurched.

'*What* were you thinking?' Muddle demanded impatiently.

'It's probably just coincidence,' said Hugo. 'But that creature looks uncannily like the Angel of the Oceans – don't you think?'

Silence.

'You have heard of the Angel of the Oceans, I take it?' asked Hugo.

'Of course,' said Muddle, frowning.

'Then you know that legend describes it as a bottle-nosed creature with flippers like giant oars?'

'Naturally.'

Rockford held his harpoon aloft.

'So you'll know that this creature brings good luck to all sailors and that, in fact, a visit from it is said to be the ultimate blessing.'

'Every sailor knows that!' snapped Muddle.

Rockford drew back his harpoon.

'Equally,' said Hugo, 'you will know that any ship that brings harm to the Angel of the Oceans will go straight to hell and sail through damnation for ever-more.'

'Drop that harpoon immediately!' yelled Oliver Muddle.

Rockford looked across with confusion etched into his forehead.

'That creature is the Angel of the Oceans,' said Muddle. 'How dare you even think of harming it?'

There was a thump and the ship lurched. The sailors all cheered.

'We are blessed.' Rusty laughed. 'The Angel of the Oceans has visited us. We are truly blessed.'

The porpoisaur swam with the boat all day. The sailors watched it dive underwater and leap high above the ocean when it surfaced, occasionally turning on to its back in mid-air. As it landed it would flick its huge tail, spraying water over everyone on the ship. Some of the crew made bets on how long their guest would remain underwater. That night the occasional thump on the ship's hull told them they still had company.

Chapter 8

'Land ahoy!'

Hugo was woken by Hawkeye shouting from the crow's nest. For a moment he thought he had dreamed it – then he heard it again.

'Land ahoy!'

He threw off his blanket and, leaving Walter sound asleep, hurried on to the main deck. But when he got out into the open air he felt horribly disappointed. The ship was sailing in the thickest fog he had ever seen. The front of the boat was completely hidden by the dense white cloud, and the sailors just a few feet away from him were ghostly silhouettes. There was no way Hawkeye would be able to see any land in the distance. He must have been playing a joke on them.

Shivering in the cold, damp air, Hugo approached some of the sailors at the bottom of the main mast. They were shouting up to Hawkeye.

'How can you see land?' said Bandit, who had lost his right arm grappling with a great white shark. 'I can't even see my cutlass in front of my face.'

'I reckon your eye is playing tricks on you,' shouted Rockford.

'Yeah,' said Swipe. 'You must be mist-taken!'

There was a thud as Hawkeye jumped the last six feet from the rigging on to the deck. The sailors stopped laughing and gathered round him. Hugo pushed between them to get to the front.

'I'm definitely not mistaken,' said Hawkeye, his eye wide with excitement. 'There's land of some sort in that there fog.'

'You're crazy,' muttered Bandit. 'You were probably holding the telescope up to your eye patch.'

Hawkeye shook his head vigorously. 'I ain't crazy. If you don't believe me, have a look for yourself.'

'What an excellent idea.' Hugo recognized Rupert's refined elocution. 'Let's have a volunteer to shin up to the crow's nest and verify Seaman Hawkeye's account.'

Hugo sensed all the sailors shuffle backwards a couple of steps. While the crew exchange glances, he looked up at the mast piercing the mist. It looked like a terrifying climb, but he was desperate to see if Hawkeye was right. He took a deep breath.

'I'll do it!' he said, taking a step forward.

'Well, well,' said Rupert. 'If it isn't our young apprentice! How very gallant of you to volunteer.'

Hugo put Hawkeye's telescope in his leather satchel and began to climb. He took slow, careful steps up the rigging, a huge grid of ropes that narrowed to a point at the very top of the mast. The rope was rough in his hands, but he held on as tightly as he could and his soft leather boots gave him a good grip. Soon he couldn't see the deck of the ship because it had been swallowed by the fog, nor could he see the top of the mast. He was alone in a murky little cocoon.

The higher he went, the more he could feel the motion of the boat – every movement was amplified, and even the gentlest rocking of the ship caused a huge, stomach-churning swing. Hugo tried not to think about his queasiness, reminding himself that he had come away in search of adventure, after all.

Looking up, he could just make out the bottom of the crow's nest. He felt relieved that he was nearly at the end of his climb, but frustrated because he still couldn't see more than a few feet through the fog. Hawkeye must have imagined seeing land.

Hugo clambered into the basket of the crow's nest and peered blindly into the murk in every direction. Then he leaned over the rim of the basket and called down to the crew.

'I can't see a thing,' he said. 'It's too foggy.'

It was a second or two before he heard Hawkeye's voice come out of the gloom. 'You're too short,' it called. 'Try standing on the barrel.'

Hugo felt around the floor of the crow's nest and found an empty beer barrel lying on its side. He stood it on its end and knelt on top of it. Then he brought his feet under him, one at a time, so that he was squatting. Slowly he started to stand up. The barrel wasn't quite even and it wobbled like a table on a cobbled street. Hugo held his arms out for balance.

As he straightened his legs and stretched his neck up, something incredible happened – his head and shoulders popped out of the mist into clear blue daylight!

The surface of the fog rose and fell gently, reminding Hugo of fresh snow on the moors at home. A memory came to him of walking in a valley with his father when the snow had thawed on all but one hilltop.

'That's the king of the hills,' Jack had told him. 'The highest peak is always the first and the last to have snow on it. It's nature's crown.'

Hugo shifted his weight as the mast swung in a wide arc from side to side, like a giant metronome. Then he saw it over his right shoulder.

A long, thin silhouette, lurking beneath the fog like a sleeping crocodile. Hugo jumped down off the crate and leaned over the side of the basket.

'Land ahoy!' he yelled triumphantly. 'Land ahoy!'

Chapter 9

Admiral Lilywhite ordered Oliver Muddle to turn the boat round. Within a few minutes the ship burst out of the smoky confusion and into the brilliant clarity of the morning. It was a beautiful day: the air was clean and the sun danced on the gently rippled surface of the ocean. His muscles swelling like balloons with the effort, Rockford operated the heavy winch that lowered the anchor.

Walter had heard Hugo shouting and got up to see what all the fuss was about. He arrived up on deck just as his nephew leaped down from the rigging.

'Uncle Walter, I saw an island!' cried Hugo, jumping up and down.

'Where?' said Walter. He peered around, blinking like a mole in the daylight.

'Hidden inside the fog!'

'Am I the first to discover this island?' said Rupert. 'Has Admiral Rupert Lilywhite indeed found virgin territory?'

'Well, well,' said Walter, smiling. 'I'm not sure. Come on, Hugo. We'd better check our charts, hadn't we?'

They went into the cabin and spread their huge map

of the ocean across the floor. For half an hour Hugo watched Walter study the chart, measuring angles and scoring lines with his quill. When Walter drew arcs Hugo watched closely, and when Walter scratched his head Hugo scratched his head too. Walter sent Hugo out to measure the angle of the sun and when he came back Walter wrote down some calculations. Finally they went back on deck.

'Well?' asked Rupert, impatiently waiting to hear their verdict. The sailors gathered around behind him.

'I've checked all our plots and double-checked all our measurements,' said Walter. He shook his head. 'And according to all official charts, there is no known land within two hundred miles of our position.'

'HOORAY!' everyone cheered.

'This calls for a celebration,' said Rupert. 'I permit everyone on the crew to have one tankard of beer.' He didn't seem to notice that the sailors were already swigging away.

'I shall call this island Rupertania and have it included on my coat of arms. We must head back to England immediately to share the news of my great discovery. Very soon everyone will know the name of the famous explorer Admiral Rupert Lilywhite, courageous discoverer of Rupertania.'

Hugo and Walter looked at each other in disbelief.

Hugo spoke first. 'Surely you're not going to sail

home without actually setting foot on the isla.
you, Admiral?' he asked incredulously.

'I don't think that's really necessary, do you?' said
Rupert.

'It *is* customary, Admiral,' said Walter. 'Normally
explorers don't consider that they've properly discovered territory without at least going ashore and having
a bit of a nose around.'

'Oh?' said Rupert with an air of disappointment.
'That seems a bit picky. I mean, I've done the hard part
by finding the place. It seems jolly unfair that I should
have all the bother of going ashore as well.'

'It's quite a good idea to bring something back from
the island to show everyone at home what an exotic
place it is,' suggested Walter. 'For instance, Columbus
brought back parrots and coconuts from the Indies.'

'So I just need to go ashore and grab a few coconuts?'
said Rupert.

'Well, the coconut has already been discovered now,'
said Walter. 'It would be better to bring back something
new that people *haven't* seen before.'

'Like what exactly?'

'I couldn't say.'

'Listen, man, there's no need to be so secretive,'
Rupert huffed.

'I can't tell you what to bring back, Admiral,' chuckled Walter, 'because I have no idea what it might be.'

'Aha!' cried Rupert with a triumphant grin. 'If you have no idea what it might be, how do you know it *isn't* a coconut?' Without waiting for a response, he turned to address the rest of the crew.

Walter looked at Hugo and shrugged.

'Excuse me, men. If I could have your attention, please,' announced Rupert. 'As you know, I have dis-covered this super island, or continent, or whatever it might be.' He paused for cheers.

Silence.

'Anyway, apparently there's some sort of technical-ity which means that before we can all go home someone has to set foot on the island. So I'd like a couple of volunteers to pop ashore and bring back a few coconuts. And please don't all shout at once.'

Hugo expected all the sailors to be desperate to have the chance to investigate an unknown land. They were such adventurous explorers, after all.

The crew examined their shoes and inspected their fingernails. A few of them started whistling. But no one volunteered. Nobody.

Eventually: 'I can't go on account of being allergic to sand,' said Rockford. 'And rowing,' he added, for good measure.

'I'd give my right arm to go and explore the island,' said Bandit. 'Unfortunately, though, I haven't got one.'

'I can't go collecting no coconuts,' said Hawkeye, 'on

account of my terrible nut allergy. I swell up ˏ
blowfish if I so much as look at a macadamia.'

Rupert was starting to get very frustrated with his
crew when Oliver Muddle asked if he could have a word
in private. He said he had thought of a solution that
would please everyone on the ship. Hugo watched the
two men whispering to each other and wondered what
they were plotting. Every now and then one of them
would glance over at him, then look away quickly when
he caught their eye. Eventually Rupert approached
Hugo and Walter. The sailors gathered behind him
again.

'The crew and I have agreed that two people should
row ashore and explore the island of Rupertania,' said
Rupert.

Walter and Hugo nodded.

'Now, clearly I am far too important to waste my
time wandering around on some deserted island trying
to find coconuts.'

Hugo couldn't help thinking Admiral Lilywhite
wasn't really embracing the whole experience of being
an explorer.

'In fact,' continued Rupert, 'it would be utter folly for
anybody to stumble blindly around the island with no
map to guide them. They could get lost, for heaven's
sake!'

Hugo and Walter looked at each other and frowned.

'So,' said Rupert, 'I am sending you two on ahead, to make a detailed map of the island. You must also pick a coconutty-type fruit or two and row back to the ship. Once we have the map, the crew and I will be equipped to explore the island without any fear of getting lost.'

Walter smiled politely. 'Admiral, Hugo and I have no way of defending ourselves. I would be happy to go ashore and record the island's landscape but I ask that some of these courageous men accompany me for protection. And I insist that Hugo stays on the ship – at least until my initial survey is complete.'

There was a metallic chime as Oliver Muddle drew his cutlass. He pointed the curved metal blade at Walter.

'I think you misunderstand Admiral Rupert,' he leered, showing off a row of shiny silver teeth.

'Seaman Muddle is right,' said Rupert. 'My plan is not a request. It is an order. Is that clear?'

'We don't have a choice, do we?' observed Hugo.

'Of course you do, laddie,' said Oliver Muddle softly. 'You can either be in that rowing boat in ten minutes, or you can walk the plank.'

Chapter 10

Hearts pounding, Walter and Hugo hurried below deck to pack essential items for their adventure, closely followed by Swipe and Rockford, who kept them within a sword's length at all times. Walter packed his map-making equipment – quills, parchment, his backstaff and measuring rope – while Hugo looked for some food. The sailors had all eaten eggs for breakfast that morning but Hugo found a few hidden under some straw at the back of the hens' cage. He wrapped them in a cloth and tucked them into his satchel, along with some biscuits and two blankets.

Before they knew it Hugo and Walter were being lowered down the side of the ship in a little wooden rowing boat. The boat hit the surface of the ocean with a slap. The sailors hauled in the pulley ropes and Walter began heaving on the oars.

'Do hurry back with my map and coconuts,' called Rupert. 'We can't hang about here forever, you know.'

As the rowing boat edged slowly back into the bank of fog Hugo and Walter watched the ship fade out of sight. Soon they were alone in the gloom.

The damp air pressed against Hugo's face and wove

its way inside his clothes. He shivered and pulled his knees up to his chest, gritting his teeth to stop them chattering.

'Well, well,' said Walter, puffing a little with the exertion of rowing. 'What an adventure we're having!' He smiled, but even in the fog Hugo could tell it wasn't his uncle's usual smile.

'Yes,' Hugo replied, his pulse racing, 'a real adventure! Just the two of us!' He grinned queasily.

'Don't worry,' said Walter. 'We'll make a basic map of the island – it won't take long. We'll be back on the ship before you can say, "Rupert needs a new brain."'

The fog disorientated Hugo as if he was wearing a blindfold. He could hear the ripple of the water against the wooden boat, but he couldn't see if they were moving. Without the reference of the sun he had no idea how long they had been in the boat – maybe an hour, maybe three. After a while he wasn't even sure if he knew which way was sky and which sea.

Suddenly the fog was behind them and they were rowing beneath clear blue skies. Walter had never seen such a sharply defined fog bank. It was like a wall of smoke across the middle of the ocean.

But Hugo was mesmerized by something else up ahead. 'There it is,' he said. His eyes were wide and his voice was high. 'There's the island. We're nearly there.'

A tall cliff of rugged black rock rose out of the ocean like a giant coalface, and as Walter rowed closer Hugo could see the waves breaking on a narrow beach of strange purple sand. The colourful cove was unlike anywhere he had ever imagined and exhilaration swept through him.

The boat lurched to a standstill as it hit the beach. Walter jumped over the bow and hauled the boat a few yards up the sand by its mooring rope. He tied the rope round a boulder and helped Hugo on to dry land.

'Isn't it incredible?' gasped Walter. 'I've never seen anything like this.'

'Me neither,' said Hugo, turning slowly round to face out to sea. 'The fog's just like a shield, hiding the island.'

'Exactly,' said Walter. 'That's probably why no one's ever discovered it before.'

'What should we do now?'

Walter tilted his head back to look up the sheer cliff face. 'Well, there's no way we can climb that, so we'd better explore the beach – see if there's another way on to the island.'

The beach was a crescent shape, fringing a shallow cove. At either end of the cove were high rocky promontories that reached into the sea like gnarly fingers. There was no way around them. And all the way along the cove the craggy cliff remained as high as the walls of Plymouth Castle.

'It's impossible,' said Walter eventually. 'We'll have to row back to the ship and report to the admiral. Either he can send some of the crew to scale the rock, or he'll have to sail round the island and look for a better place to go ashore.'

'Do we have to go straight back?' said Hugo. 'Can't we stay for a while? It's so exciting feeling like we're real explorers at last.'

Walter's instincts told him the safest option was to head back to the ship. He looked around at the beach. All seemed quiet and still. Then he looked at his nephew's eager expression.

'Fine,' he said. 'We'll spend a couple of hours here. But then we're going straight back to the boat.'

'Hooray!' whooped Hugo. 'Let's build a campfire.'

He pulled off his boots and ran barefoot down the beach, leaving a trail of footprints in the purple sand.

CHapter 11

Hugo and Walter found a rock pool and caught two crabs the size of saucers. They built a small fire from driftwood and pierced the crabs' shells with sticks before holding them over the flames. Neither spoke for a long time. The only sounds were the shushing of the ocean and the crackle of the campfire.

Walter took his crab out of the fire, snapped off a pincer and laid it on a rock. Cracking open the shell, he pulled out a piece of white meat the size of his thumb and gave it to Hugo. It was soft and sweet and seemed to melt on his tongue.

'Oh, it's delicious!' he said. 'So tender. And it hasn't even got any bones.'

Walter's moustache twitched. 'Well, it beats boiling turnips for our tea, that's for sure.'

When they had devoured the meat of both crabs Hugo and Walter lay back on the sand.

'Last night I dreamed I was the first explorer to reach India by sea,' said Hugo. 'I've studied your maps – if you sailed the right course, I think you could leave Plymouth and be in India within six months.'

'England to India in six months?' Walter whistled.

'I'm not sure travel is *ever* going to be quite that quick.'

'Well, what continent do you think we are on now?' asked Hugo.

'I don't know,' said Walter. 'We are further north than Columbus sailed. As you know, though, I don't think he'd sailed far enough to reach India. His passage was blocked by an unknown continent.'

'How many continents do you think there are?'

'Well, that's the sixty-four-thousand-sovereign question,' said Walter. 'But I think we are on the verge of finding out. This is such a wonderful time for exploration. The world has existed for millions of years, but only now do we have the ships and the knowledge to be able to navigate across vast oceans. Da Gama claims he'll soon be the first man to sail to India – if you don't beat him to it.'

'He'll have to be quick.' Hugo gave his uncle a gappy smile.

'Our understanding of the world is improving at an incredible rate,' said Walter. 'We are fortunate to have the chance to play our part.' His voice dropped to a whisper. 'Maps are the key that will unlock the world, Hugo. When the world map is complete, anything will be possible. With reliable charts to guide them, I see no reason why someone couldn't actually sail all the way round the world one day.'

Hugo's eyes were round. 'And maybe, one day, ordinary people will travel across oceans just to visit other countries for themselves,' he said.

'Your imagination is quite something, Hugo,' said Walter, his moustache twitching again. 'Next you'll be telling me that one day a man will sail a magic ship to the moon.'

Hugo blushed and sat quietly for a moment. He brushed his fringe from his forehead and frowned. 'So right now we could be on a little island or a whole new continent?'

Walter nodded. 'One thing's for sure though. It doesn't exist on any maps I've ever seen.'

Hugo took a deep breath. The air was clean. No sewers or sweaty crowds here.

'It's so peaceful,' he said. 'It seems a shame to spoil it all by bringing scores of traders here.'

'We can't keep it a secret forever,' smiled Walter.

'Can't we at least spend the night here – just the two of us?' pleaded Hugo. 'It's like paradise.'

Their bonfire was dwindling. The flames had died and the embers hissed gently. The sun was dipping into the sea and the sky was blood red and inky blue.

'Just one night then,' agreed Walter. He was happy to indulge his nephew's enthusiasm, but the truth was that his own sense of adventure was beginning to stir. It had been a long time since his fingers had tingled with such anticipation. 'We'll have to get some more wood for this fire though. Otherwise we'll freeze to dea—'

His last word was drowned out by an ear-piercing squawk overhead. It echoed hauntingly off the rock, then seemed to disappear out to sea. Walter and Hugo froze.

There was another squawk, then a third. Then came a slow, rhythmic flapping sound. It was like a ship's sail snapping taut in the wind, followed by a long silence. Then a couple more flaps, then silence again. Instinctively Walter jumped to his feet. As he scanned the sky, he felt for Hugo and pulled him upright.

The silhouettes of three winged creatures passed overhead in lazy circles. Although the flight pattern was similar to that of kestrels and hawks, these were no ordinary birds. Hugo couldn't tell how close they were, but just by the rhythm of their motion he knew they were big. He estimated they had a wingspan of possibly three times his own height. When the setting sun caught the outlines of their heads, he gasped. They had stubby snouts instead of beaks.

Every now and then they would stop circling and come to hover, beating their broad wings to stay aloft.

'What *are* they?' asked Hugo, cowering.

'Some kind of hunting bird,' said Walter.

'So . . . what are they hunting?'

Walter grabbed Hugo's wrist and started pulling him up the beach towards the cliff.

'Us . . . run!'

CHapter 12

One of the monstrous birds dived. With its wings tucked by its side it dropped head first towards its fleeing prey. Suddenly sleek, it pierced the evening air in a flash. It was a natural hunter, and its eyesight was as sharp as its claws.

Surveying the two figures scurrying along the sand like beetles, instinct told it that the smaller prey would be easier to catch and easier to kill. Its wings remained tucked back until it was just a few feet above its target. In a fraction of an instant it spread them wide, fanned its huge feathers and flapped hard to arrest its descent. At the same time it rotated its body, allowing its legs to hang down as if it was coming in to land.

As it came to a hover its claws stretched wide, like the mouth of a chick anticipating a meal. Its judgement was perfect. It could feel the small figure's shoulders lightly touching its talons. Then its claws snatched shut.

Hugo tripped on a rock and fell to his knees. He felt something snag the back of his shirt, then he was free. Walter pulled him to his feet. Feeling some powerful blasts of air, as if there was a giant bellows above him, he looked up. The sky was obscured by a vast spread of feathers. Immediately above his head, the bird-like creature was climbing away, its wings snapping hard as it hauled itself high into the sky.

It would be a few moments before the beast realized that it was empty-clawed. Pale-faced, Hugo realized that the stumble had saved him for sure.

Hugo and Walter ran to the cliff and pressed their backs as flat to the rocks as they could, keeping their eyes fixed on their attackers circling overhead. As they edged along the rock they felt for any cracks or nooks that might offer some kind of cover.

'Are they giant eagles?' whispered Hugo, squinting at the sky.

Walter shook his head. 'Not necessarily. The species here could be like nothing we've ever seen before.'

Another of the birds dived. This time Walter saw it coming and pushed Hugo behind him. The black missile accelerated towards Walter, suddenly dropping its lethal talons. He put a hand up to protect his face and felt the claws grip his forearm. The monster bird flapped its wings furiously and for the first time Hugo could see it up close. Its body and wings were covered in blue-black feathers, but its head was like a huge rat's, with a bulbous black eye on each side and two teeth protruding from the front of its pointed snout. As it hissed, a long black tongue wormed out of its mouth and licked at Walter's face like a flame.

Walter desperately dug his heels into the sand, sinking as low as he could get. But as the rat-bird beat its powerful wings he could feel the ground slipping from under him.

The flying rat's snout snarled up and it began to shriek. For one crazy moment it sounded to Hugo like the beast was screaming, 'You're mine, you're mine, you're mine!'

Thinking quickly, Hugo snatched up a log about the size of his arm and, holding the thinner end of the wood in his hand, he swung it above his head with all his strength as if it was an axe. The log came down on the back of the rat-bird's neck, provoking a hideous squawk and a swift vertical retreat, minus its prey.

With a sigh of relief, Hugo helped his uncle to his feet and they both pressed themselves against the rock. As Walter ran his hands over the cliff face he found a crevice, about twelve inches across and three feet high.

'Quickly,' he ordered. 'Hide in here.'

Hugo ducked into the crack head first. Turning sideways, he pushed an arm and a leg into the narrow opening. Then, wriggling and grunting, he managed to squeeze the rest of his body through the tiny gap and pulled his satchel in after him. He was surprised to discover that the space opened out into a narrow cave that he could stand up in.

'Come in,' he called to Walter. 'There's plenty of room.'

Grimacing with effort, Walter pushed his head into the low opening. He reached in with one arm, his fingers scrabbling at the rock as he tried in vain to force the rest of his body through.

'It's no good,' sighed Uncle Walter eventually. 'I'll have to find somewhere else.'

At that moment his expression changed. A look of surprise appeared briefly on his face, before changing again into something like sadness. Or maybe it was defeat.

Then he jerked backwards out of the crevice, as if yanked by some invisible force. He fell flat on to the ground, hitting the sand with a thwack.

Watching in horror, Hugo saw that one of the rat-birds had grabbed hold of his uncle. The old man twisted violently on the sand, then turned upside down as his feet were hoisted above his head.

Walter caught Hugo's eye for a second.

'Hugo! Don't worry about the map, just get home safely,' he shouted. 'Row back to the ship immediately!'

Before Hugo could reply, Uncle Walter was hauled off the ground and out of sight. Hugo pressed one eye to the crevice to catch a final glimpse of him. The rat-bird was already in the distance, climbing up into the night sky. The claws of one foot were clamped round Uncle

Walter's ankle, lifting him high over the cliff and towards the interior of the island. Hugo watched until his uncle was out of sight. Sickened, he sat down, alone in the pitch-black cavern. Alone in the world.

Chapter 13

Hugo shivered with cold and fear. He wished his parents were with him now. No – actually, he wished he was at home with them, just like years ago. When he closed his eyes he could see them as clearly as ever.

His mother was a small woman with chestnut-coloured curls and kind brown eyes. His father was tall and lean with straight fair hair and blue eyes, and he worked in his workshop – a wooden shack next to their house. Hugo would spend hours watching him sawing, planing and carving. His father's mind was as agile as his hands and while he worked he would make up riddles for Hugo to solve. When Jack wasn't working he would take Hugo walking in the countryside and teach him about plants and wildlife. In the evenings, Hugo would listen to his father recount fantastic stories of his brother Walter's travels to far-off places.

Gripping his wooden pendant now, he remembered his father teaching him to play chess, and one particular occasion when he had lost most of his pieces and had grown frustrated.

'I give in,' he'd said grumpily.

'The game isn't finished yet,' his father had replied.

'But I'll lose anyway, so what's the point in playing on?'

'The point is that you may win. A pawn and a knight can beat a whole army of pieces if they're used wisely,' his father had said. 'You must never give up until the game is over.'

When he had been sent to the workhouse Hugo had felt more alone than ever. But every morning he drew strength from picturing his father giving his familiar advice. Hugo's resolve had paid off when Walter finally returned from his voyage. Walter had rescued Hugo on that occasion – now it was time to return the favour.

Hugo felt a surge of determination. So the situation he was in was decidedly sticky. He was alone in the middle of the ocean. On a strange island inhabited by flying rats. Who happened to have taken his uncle and sole companion. But he wasn't beaten yet. His uncle might still be alive and, as long as there was a chance he could be saved, Hugo would never give up trying.

Despite Walter's instructions, he wouldn't go back to the ship yet. If Admiral Lilywhite got wind of the bizarre birds on the island, he would surely flee back to England as fast as his sails could carry him. Then Hugo would never see Uncle Walter again. No, Hugo decided, if he wanted someone to rescue his uncle from the feathered fiends, he was going to have to do it himself.

'You *are* meant to be Honest, Undaunted, Gallant and Optimistic,' he reminded himself.

Now that his eyes were beginning to get accustomed to the darkness, he made a small pile of wood in the cave and pushed dried seaweed between the sticks to act as kindling. Then he took two rocks and banged them together close to the seaweed. Eventually a spark caught and the flames began to smoulder. Soon he had built himself a nice little campfire.

Just as he was getting toasty a loud squawk echoed round the cave. As it reverberated around him Hugo once again thought he recognized human words.

'You're trapped, you're trapped,' it seemed to say. Then, 'You're mine, mine, you're mine.'

Hugo was sure his mind was playing tricks on him – wasn't it? He jumped up and ran to the entrance, then stopped in his tracks: one of the bird-rat-monster things was trying to get into the cave. Its hairy head and feathery shoulders were through the gap already. When it saw Hugo it bared its teeth, allowing its tongue to weave out of its mouth and probe into the cave. This time there was no mistaking its cry.

'You're mine, you're mine,' it hissed.

For a moment Hugo was frozen by terror and disbelief. What sort of fantastic island was this?

But he had no time to dwell on the matter. The monster was wriggling hard and would soon be in the cave with him. Instinctively he grabbed a stick from the fire and waved it at the intruder like a flaming sabre.

'I'm *not* yours,' he shouted as the rat-bird scrabbled backwards. Hugo jabbed the flame at it until it was gone.

'So you don't like fire, huh?' he muttered. He took a couple of burning sticks from the existing fire. After propping them up at the mouth of the cavern he set about collecting more wood.

One piece was shaped just like the paddle of an oar that had rotted over time. He laid it on the fire and was just about to throw on another, smaller piece when he noticed that this second piece had some kind of writing on it. Using the firelight for illumination, he studied the characters on the wood.

Hugo had never seen any letters or symbols like these before. Maybe the strange alphabet spelt out a word! It might be the name of a foreign ship that had perished on the rocky coastline or a dying message from someone else who'd been trapped in the cave. But who might have been here before him, and where would they have come from? More importantly, where were they now?

Intrigued by his discovery, he placed the wood inside his satchel, under the blankets. When the second bonfire was roaring away at the cave's entrance, Hugo went deep inside the cave and lay down.

Staring at the ceiling of the cave he tried to imagine what a map of this bizarre territory would look like. How would the coastline develop beyond the thin crescent of the purple beach, and what sort of terrain would be detailed beyond the ridge of the black cliffs?

And what warnings to travellers would the map's legend contain – apart from the one that would read *Beware the flying rats*?

Chapter 14

Hugo woke up feeling startled and hungry. Both his campfires had died. He had no idea how long he'd been sleeping without the protection of the flames. It was daylight outside his cave and the ashes of the fire were cool.

With his satchel over his shoulder he crawled through the cave's opening until he could just see outside. Everything was still. When he was sure that there were no monsters circling overhead he squeezed through the crevice and on to the beach.

The thick fog bank echoed the shape of the shoreline just a short distance out to sea. The beach was as peaceful as it had been when he had cooked crabs with Uncle Walter the previous night. The memory of that idyllic supper brought a lump to Hugo's throat. How dramatically their fortunes had changed.

He knew he would have to climb the rocky cliff if he was going to find his uncle. Pressing one foot on to a tiny lump – it was no more than a pimple on the cliff face – he hauled himself off the ground. He reached up for a handhold and felt with his other foot for something to stand on. Eventually he found another foothold and tried to pull himself up another step. This time his foot slipped. He fell flat against the cliff and dropped to the sand in a heap.

He tried again and again, but the black rock was too smooth. Every time he came crashing back down to the beach.

'This is hopeless,' Hugo mumbled angrily. 'I'll never climb these rocks.'

'You can do it,' said a quiet voice.

Hugo spun round and scanned the empty beach, his heart galloping. 'Who said that?'

'I did.'

Still Hugo could see no one.

'Down here.'

When he looked down a tiny movement caught his eye. There was a creature on the sand about the size of a mouse. It had soft white fur with a flash of black running from the tip of its nose to its tail. Its floppy ears were bald and translucent, like the pink skin of a newborn hamster, and strangely large: each as big as its head. The creature sat up on its haunches, tucking its paws in. A long hairless tail trailed out behind it. Above its whiskery pink nose, two beady eyes blinked at Hugo.

Hugo picked up a twig and crouched down on the sand. His hand trembled as he extended his arm towards the animal.

The creature opened its mouth and Hugo could see tiny teeth like the tips of needles in its mouth.

'I hope you're not thinking of poking me with that stick,' it said in a voice that was firm and not at all squeaky.

Hugo jumped so high that he lost his balance and fell back on to his bottom. Frantically he scrambled backwards until his shoulders were up against the rock face. He stared at the mouse-like creature, his eyes swollen with disbelief and fear.

'What are you staring at? Do I have seaweed on my snout or something?' asked the animal, going cross-eyed trying to look at its own nose.

'No,' Hugo heard himself say. 'Your snout is fine – perfectly clean.'

'It's my ears, isn't it? You're staring at my ears.'

Hugo could hardly breathe. 'No,' he said. 'I just can't believe that you can talk.'

'Of course I can talk,' said the animal. 'I might have ridiculous ears, but I'm not dumb.'

Hugo wondered if he'd bumped his head last night and lost his senses. Then he remembered the squawks of the birds. He closed his eyes tight and shook his head. 'Come on, Hugo,' he said out loud. 'Pull yourself together.'

He opened his eyes and looked down at the animal.

'Yes, pull yourself together, Hugo,' said the floppy-eared mouse. 'Things are never as bad as they seem. I'm having the worst morning ever, but I'm not letting it get me down.'

'Why? What's happened to you?' asked Hugo, trying to overlook the fact that he was talking to a mouse.

The little animal spoke quickly. 'I was minding my own business when my friend asked me if I fancied a ride on his back while he flew out to get some food. Next thing I knew, he was showing off doing aerobatics and I couldn't hold on. How the fall didn't kill me I'll never know. I've been here for hours, trying to find a way up those rocks. I saw you struggling to climb them too so I thought you could do with some encouragement, but then you tried to impale me with a twig.'

'I'm really sorry,' said Hugo. 'I wasn't going to hurt you.'

'Lucky for you,' remarked the tiny rodent. 'If you'd come any closer, I'd have knocked you out.'

A giggle escaped from Hugo's mouth before he could stop it.

'I'm serious,' said the mouse. 'I am the strongest creature on this island.'

'You?' said Hugo.

'Absolutely,' said the little creature, puffing its chest out and extending its tail to its full length. Then it mumbled something about mice eyes.

'Sorry?' said Hugo. 'What have mice eyes got to do with you being strong?'

'Hmm?'

'Did you say "four mice eyes"?'

'No.'

'That's what it sounded like.'

'Oh.'

'So what *did* you say?'

'I said "for my size",' said the animal sheepishly, the tips of its ears turning bright pink. 'I said, "I am the strongest creature on this island – *for my size.*"'

'But you're tiny,' said Hugo with a smile.

'What's your point?'

Hugo decided to change the subject. 'So why didn't your friend pick you up after dropping you?'

'He's probably looking for me on the clifftop, the silly old flutterhog. I've tried to call him, but he can't hear me.'

'Do you think he'll realize you're down here?'

'Definitely. Eventually. I mean probably. Come to think of it, maybe not.' The animal sighed. 'Anyway, how did you get here?'

'On a boat,' said Hugo. 'I came with my uncle, but a flying rat took him away.'

'A scavagor? They're such lowlifes.'

'That's why I have to climb these rocks – to rescue him from those flea-ridden monsters.'

'That's the spirit,' said the animal, clenching its two front paws. 'You must never give up.'

'Hey – that's what my father used to tell me,' said Hugo.

'I'd like to teach those flying freaks a lesson or two myself,' said the black-and-white mouse.

'You know, a pawn and a knight can defeat a whole army.'

'Pardon?' The creature blinked at Hugo.

'Oh, it's just something else my father used to say,' Hugo said. 'Why don't you hop into my pocket and we'll see if we can find your friend too?'

'I'm in – as long as I can be the knight.'

'Be my guest,' said Hugo.

The mouse scampered up Hugo's leg and leaped into his tunic pocket. A moment later its head popped back up.

'By the way, I'm savage.'

'Let me guess,' said Hugo. 'For your size you are the most savage creature on the island?'

'No. That's my name. Savage.'

'Oh. Pleased to meet you.'

'Do you mind if I just have a little doze? It's so cosy in here and I'm exhausted after trying to clamber up those rocks all morning. Besides, I need to conserve my energy for when we take on the scavagors.'

Before Hugo could answer, Savage disappeared back into his pocket and closed the flap behind him.

Hugo moved along the beach a few yards to try

another part of the rock. As he ran his hands over the cliff he felt a rough surface that wasn't like the rest of the rock. It seemed to run all the way to the top of the cliff like a vein. He tugged it away from the cliff with all his strength. It was a rope! With a crack and a twang it came unstuck from the cliff face but remained securely attached at the top.

Holding the rope with both hands, Hugo leaned back and, taking his weight with his arms, started edging his way towards the top of the cliff.

After some time he came to a ledge about three feet deep. His arms were tired and he was hungry, so he pulled himself on to the ledge. Gently he lifted the flap of his tunic pocket and peeked in. Savage was curled into a furry ball, purring softly in his sleep. Hugo took a biscuit out of his satchel and sat down to eat with his feet dangling. The black rock and the purple sand far below made for a stunning view but he was impatient to keep going.

As Hugo stood to continue his ascent, the blood in his limbs chilled. He couldn't believe he hadn't seen it before. Lying on the ledge just a few feet away from him like a great big sack of feathers was a scavagor – fast asleep. It was lying on its side, its ugly head sprawled across the floor. Its mouth was wide open and its slippery tongue trailed across the ledge like an eel.

Hugo panicked and felt for the rope. In his hurry to

escape he kicked some loose rocks, which clunked noisily down the cliff. The scavagor's eyes opened wide. It
sprang to its claws in a flash of feathers.

The rope was just beyond Hugo's grasp. He heard the
beat of the creature's wings as it lunged. He felt the
tickle of a tongue lick his ear. He backed away from the
rock face and, before he could grab the rope, he was
falling. His body twisted so that he was plummeting
head first. The air rushed past his ears and his satchel
buffeted noisily behind him as he thrashed his arms
and kicked his legs. All he could see was purple sand
rushing up to meet him.

This is it, Hugo thought. Now the game is over.

Chapter 15

Something grabbed Hugo's shoulders and pulled him upward. His whole body was stretched tight as he was hauled out of his freefall. Then he was hanging limply in the breeze like washing pegged out on a line.

Another scavagor must have snatched him. He imagined being taken to its nest and fed to its young in small bite-size pieces, with Savage being served as dessert. He decided he'd rather drop to the rocks below than end up as a bird's breakfast, so he started to struggle. He kicked his legs and twisted his body. He punched his fists blindly above his head as hard as he could.

'Let go of me, you ugly, rat-faced freak,' he shouted. 'I won't let you eat me. I won't.'

'My dear boy,' said a voice above Hugo's head, 'who are you calling ugly? And, just for the record, I'd rather eat my own hair than snack on a skinny little squirm like you. Now do keep still, there's a good fellow. If you keep flapping around like that, I'll be forced to hand you back to the scavagors.'

'But aren't you a scavagor?' asked Hugo, who had stopped punching now.

'Goodness me, no,' said the voice. 'Scavagors are the

flying vermin that you were trying to evade when you fell off the cliff. I've never seen anything quite so inept as your attempt to escape, by the way. An elephant playing a drum would have caused less commotion than you did.'

Embarrassed, Hugo dangled in silence for a minute. But he was too fascinated by this new talking creature to be quiet for long.

'So, if you're not a scavagor, what does that make you?' he asked.

'Have a look for yourself,' said the voice. 'Pull yourself up and climb aboard,'

Hugo twisted his body and reached up, grabbing hold of the fur on the creature's shoulder. He clambered up its flank and slung a leg over its back. When he was sitting firmly astride the creature he grabbed two fistfuls of coarse hair and held on tight.

'Well?' said the creature. 'What do I look like to you?'

Hugo examined his mount from tip to tail before speaking. It had a big round belly and four skinny little legs. Yellow splodges on its pink skin showed through its thin coat of coarse black hair. At its rear it had a short, curly tail.

'You're very unusual,' he noted.

'I'm more than unusual,' said the animal. 'I'm unique.'

Hugo looked at the small wings flapping furiously on

either side of him. 'Your wings are like a humming-bird's. They're quite small, aren't they?'

'I prefer the term "petite",' replied the animal. 'And what about my face? How would you describe that?'

The animal turned its head proudly – first to the left, then to the right – so that Hugo could see its profile. He examined it carefully. It had two flappy ears covered in black hair, and two small eyes set low in its fat cheeks. And it had a short, squashed snout complete with two twitching and dribbling nostrils. It wasn't the prettiest animal Hugo had ever seen by a long way.

'Well,' it persisted, 'what do you think?'

'You're a bit like . . .' said Hugo nervously. 'I mean, from some angles you look a bit . . .'

'Go on. Just say it.'

'Well, you're really quite piggy,' Hugo blurted out.

For a moment there was silence. Hugo wondered if he'd hurt the animal's feelings.

'Gosh. Piggy, eh?' said the animal proudly. 'Thank you. I am so pleased that you find me so handsome.'

'I didn't say . . .' Hugo stopped himself.

'So, what's your name?' asked the animal. It was puffing hard now and Hugo thought maybe its wings were flapping with a little less vigour.

'Hugo. What's yours?'

'I am Pigasus,' said the animal. 'It's very nice to catch up with you, Hugo. I don't suppose you've seen a little mousy fellow with impossibly large ears? I sort of dropped him off here a little while ago.'

Hugo had forgotten all about his passenger. 'Let me think,' he said, smiling to himself. He reached into his pocket and tickled the warm furry tummy. A moment later Savage's beady eyes were peering up at him from beneath the pocket's flap.

'How's it going?' asked Savage.

'See for yourself.'

Savage pushed his head out of Hugo's pocket and looked around. 'Pigasus!' he cried.

'Savage!' said Pigasus, turning his head and grinning. 'I thought I'd lost you.'

'You did lose me,' said Savage sulkily.

'I seem to remember that you fell off my back.'

'You dropped me.'

'I did tell you to hang on.'

'You didn't tell me you were about to turn upside down,' said Savage, scampering up Hugo's arm and perching on his shoulder. 'Luckily Hugo here rescued me.'

'Well, I rescued Hugo,' said Pigasus. 'So technically I rescued you too.'

'I think that makes you even,' said Hugo.

Savage and Pigasus scowled at each other for a moment. Then Savage leaped on to Pigasus's head.

'I forgive you,' said Savage, scratching his friend's ear.

'Apology accepted,' said Pigasus, between snorts of pleasure. 'Now let's head for home.'

'Er . . . where exactly are we going?' asked Hugo.

'We're going to meet some friends on the other side of the island,' said Pigasus. 'Don't worry about the scavagors – they can't fly in the daytime because the sun saps their strength. So sit back, relax and enjoy the view.'

'But we have to find my uncle,' insisted Hugo. 'The scavagors snatched him last night.'

'That's terrible news.' Pigasus sighed. 'But I think I know someone who might be able to help.'

Pigasus climbed higher and higher into the morning sky. Out to sea Hugo could see beyond the fog bank to where *El Tonto Perdido* was anchored. He could just see the top of its mast swaying from side to side, and he wondered if Hawkeye was watching them from the crow's nest. Pigasus would look just like a normal bird from that distance, Hugo thought.

As they turned and flew inland Hugo noticed that the ground sloped down from the clifftop, like the rim of a plate. The island was covered in beautiful green grass that looked like velvet from Hugo's seat in the sky. Soon they were flying over a dense band of trees that grew in a perfect circle, forming a ring of forest that took up half the island.

'That's Tanglefoot Forest,' said Pigasus, gasping and sweating as the trees passed beneath him. 'If you fall off here, don't expect me to come and find you.'

'Is it dangerous?' said Hugo.

'No, it's a really fun place to relax and hang out.'

'Really?'

'No,' snorted Pigasus. 'I was being sarcastic. It's home to the nastiest, most evil, most vicious creatures on the island – much worse than the scavagors. Anyone who goes in there will probably never come out alive. You wouldn't get me down there for all the rotten fruit in the world.'

'I see,' said Hugo, holding on a little more tightly.

By the time they were clear of the forest, Pigasus was wheezing hard and his little wings were definitely slow-ing down. They were no longer just a blur and Hugo could make out their black and gold feathers.

'Are you all right?' asked Hugo, patting Pigasus's head gently.

'You're not as young as you used to be, are you, Piga-sus?' chuckled Savage.

'I'm fine,' said Pigasus, between gasps. 'Just a little tired, that's all. These wings of mine weren't made to carry others. They're far too small.'

'Oh, I wouldn't call them small,' said Hugo. 'Just petite.'

Pigasus turned his head and smiled. 'I can see we're going to be friends,' he said.

Soon Hugo realized that Pigasus was descending. Tanglefoot Forest was behind them and the ground down below was sloping gently up.

'Hold tight, we're about to land,' said Pigasus. 'I've never quite got the hang of this bit.'

'I think this might be a good time for me to snuggle down in your pocket again,' remarked Savage. The little rodent jumped in and burrowed down deep.

'I think he's asleep again,' said Hugo, seconds later.

'Probably,' gasped Pigasus. 'He's the only creature I know that sleeps even more than I do.'

He swooped down towards the ground, Hugo holding on with all his strength. As thick emerald leaves whipped past their heads, Pigasus started running in mid-air. A moment later his trotters met the earth and he was charging along the ground, trying to slow down.

For a moment Hugo thought everything was going to be fine. Then Pigasus caught his hoof on a low branch. Falling flat on to his tummy, he slid along the grass at great speed. He pirouetted slowly, with his four legs spread out wide, flattening saplings and squashing

flowers as he went. Finally he came to a halt with his head stuck in a very thorny bramble bush.

'Are you all right?' gasped Hugo, who had been terrified throughout the entire crash-landing.

'Absolutely tickety boo,' said Pigasus, pulling his head out of the brambles. 'Although, between you and me, for a moment there I thought everything was going to go horribly wrong.'

'You mean it didn't?'

'Oh no,' said Savage, his whiskery nose protruding from Hugo's pocket. 'That was one of his smoother touchdowns.'

'Did you have fun?' said Pigasus.

'Oh, er, yes,' said Hugo. 'It was one of the best flights I've ever had.'

'How many flights have you had exactly?' asked Pigasus.

'Just the one,' said Hugo, giggling, 'but it was definitely in my top five.'

They were standing at the foot of another rock face. It was almost completely sheer with a sharp ragged ridge way up in the clouds. Pigasus paused and surveyed the undergrowth, his snout twitching and his ears pricked up. Satisfied they were alone, he took Hugo through a narrow gap in some bushes that led them into a tunnel through the rock. After lots of twisting and turning they came out into a clearing in a wood.

'That was all very secretive,' observed Hugo.

'It's supposed to be,' said Pigasus. 'The ridge forms a sort of natural wall. It completely cuts off this peninsula, which we call Shelter Point. It's about the safest place on the island. They can't get to us here.'

'Who can't?'

'The buffalogres,' said Pigasus ominously. 'Wait here. I'm just going to tell the others that we have a guest. I'll only be gone a few minutes.'

'I'll come with you,' said Savage, scrambling out of Hugo's pocket. In three bounds he was perched on top of Pigasus's head.

Before Hugo could ask who or what the buffalogres were, Pigasus had trotted away.

Much sooner than Hugo had expected – almost immediately, in fact – he heard footsteps approaching. He wanted to make a good impression on Pigasus and Savage's friends, so he straightened his clothes and flattened his hair – the way his mother used to do to him when they went to visit relatives.

It was only when he heard a twig snap behind him that Hugo realized he was waiting at the wrong path. He turned to see a figure emerge from the tunnel they'd just exited. And it wasn't one of his new friends.

Hugo was sharing the clearing with something that was about twice the size of Pigasus, quite a lot hairier and not half as friendly-looking.

Panic-stricken, Hugo stood still. The bear-like creature lumbered around the clearing without seeing him. Standing about eight feet tall, it was a mountain of shaggy silver fur. The beast had long powerful arms and stocky legs supporting its hulking body. Small tufty ears stood on top of its round head and its long snout tapered into a blunt brown nose.

Hugo watched its leathery nostrils twitch. It sniffed the air twice. The hair on the animal's muscular shoulders bristled like an angry cat as its head snapped round to point at Hugo. He couldn't see the creature's eyes under its silver fringe, but he knew they were locked on to him. Its snout peeled open to reveal two rows of sharp fangs. A rattling snarl echoed off the rock.

Was *this* a buffalogre?

Petrified, Hugo waited for the beast to pounce. He knew it was just a matter of seconds before this animal savaged him.

But the creature didn't pounce. Instead it slowly reached an arm behind its own head. Its huge palms were black and leathery with short, stubby fingers – halfway between a hand and a paw. Before Hugo could wonder what it was doing, the animal drew a mighty sword from a sheath on its back. With its arm and the blade making one perfectly straight line, the figure pointed the sword at Hugo. The tip of the weapon was almost touching his nose.

In a whisper the beast said something to itself. It sounded like, 'Not again.'

Then with two paws the creature raised the sword over his head.

Chapter 16

'NO!'

Hugo heard the voice but he didn't know who it had come from. His eyes were transfixed by the sword that was threatening to chop him in half at any moment. At the root of the blade he could make out a carving of an acorn.

'He's only a child. He can't mean us any harm.'

Hugo still didn't dare take his eyes off the blade, but he was sure the voice didn't belong to Pigasus or Savage. It sounded like a young girl.

'We don't know who he is,' bellowed the big silver-haired creature without lowering the sword.

'Well, why don't you ask him?'

For just a split second Hugo looked away from the sword and glanced at the approaching figure.

He had been right to think the voice belonged to a girl. She was about his height and her face was almost the shape of a human's, except that she had no nostrils or eyebrows. Long shiny hair tumbled down to her hips and she had the biggest green eyes Hugo had ever seen. Her skin was smooth and pale blue, the colour of the sky on a clear winter's day.

'Hello,' she said.

'Hello,' said Hugo, looking back at the sword again.

'Don't worry,' she said. 'He won't hurt you.'

Hugo felt he could trust the girl. She gave him a quick smile and her pretty eyes shone like fresh green apples.

'What's your name?' she asked.

'I'm Hugo.'

'Hello, Hugo,' she said. 'I'm Delphina and this is Snowdon.'

Hugo nodded to them both, still eyeing Snowdon suspiciously.

'How did you get here?' she asked.

'Well, I came on a ship with an explorer.' At this Snowdon growled and stiffened. Delphina put a hand on his paw and this seemed to settle him. Hugo noticed that her fingers were webbed, like a duck's foot. He continued, 'This explorer, well, he wouldn't even come on the island. I think he was scared, or maybe just lazy. Or both.'

'Scared and lazy,' repeated Delphina. 'That doesn't sound like a very good combination for an explorer.'

'It isn't.' Hugo grinned. 'He's about the worst explorer in the world. He sent me and my uncle ashore to make a map for him so he wouldn't get lost.'

'And where's your uncle now?'

'He was taken away – by the scavagors.' Suddenly

Hugo felt exhausted and very sad. Snowdon lowered his sword and slid it back into the scabbard on his back. Delphina rested a webbed hand on Hugo's shoulder. 'How did you find us?'

'I came with Pigasus,' said Hugo, feeling brighter. 'And Savage.'

'Really? Where are they then?' said Snowdon.

Before Hugo could answer, he heard Pigasus calling his name from beyond the bushes.

'Hugo! Hugo! Sorry – that took longer than expected. We just got a little bit sidetracked, I'm afraid.'

Then Pigasus appeared, waddling on his two hind legs and cradling a pile of peaches in his arms. Savage was sitting on top of the pile, gnawing hungrily on one of the fruits.

'I found all these peaches under a tree just up there and I couldn't resist,' said Pigasus, his snout covered in juice and pieces of peach flesh. He snuffled down another peach before offering a particularly brown-looking one to Hugo. 'Want one?'

'It looks a bit rotten,' said Hugo, wrinkling his nose.

'I know,' said Pigasus. 'That's exactly how I like them. Fancy a peach, Delphina?'

Delphina shook her head. 'No, thank you, Pigasus. I prefer my fruit a little less mashed.'

Pigasus shrugged and tossed the peach into the air before catching it in his mouth. 'Well, I see you've met my new friend, Hugo,' he said, spraying juice over the others.

'He says the scavagors have taken his uncle,' said Snowdon. His voice was surprisingly quiet for such a big creature, but it burbled with potential menace.

Pigasus nodded sympathetically.

'Do you think he's still alive?' said Hugo.

Delphina put an arm round him. 'Before we talk about that, let's see if we can find you some food that isn't riddled with maggots.'

Snowdon grunted and led the way through the woods.

'I don't think he's very pleased to see me,' whispered Hugo.

'Don't take it personally,' Delphina replied. 'He's very friendly once you get to know him. It's just that he hasn't seen a human for some time.'

'You mean humans have been here before me?' said Hugo.

'Just one,' said Delphina. 'But he betrayed our trust.'

'In what way?'

Delphina laughed and shook her head. 'You have so many questions. I'm sure Pigasus and Snowdon will tell you everything over supper. But it'll be dark soon and we need to build a fire before the light fades – otherwise we may have some very dangerous company.'

'I thought Shelter Point was safely hidden away behind the ridge.'

She sighed. 'Nowhere is completely safe on this island.'

Chapter 17

Hugo sat cross-legged, staring at the plate on his lap. Supper was a strange feast of giant eel, roasted and served with some kind of weird vegetable that Pigasus had dug up. It was about the size of a fist, with a thick brown skin on the outside, soft and white inside. Snowdon called it a patata.

'So,' said Hugo, clearing his throat and putting down his plate, 'do you think there's any chance that my uncle is still alive?' He scanned the faces around the fire for any hint of optimism.

'Listen, Hugo,' said Pigasus gently. 'Let me explain to you how the scavagors work.'

Hugo held his breath.

'The scavagors are the vermin of this island. They fly around at night looking for vulnerable animals they can capture and take into Tanglefoot Forest. They usually prey on young animals – babies and cubs. They were probably trying to snatch you when they got your uncle by mistake.'

Hugo swallowed hard. 'Why would they take him into the forest?'

'Because they are cowards,' said Pigasus, chewing on

a rather large slice of eel. 'The scavagors are nasty and ugly, but they are like every other creature on this island in one way – they live in fear of the buffalogres. They sacrifice anything they catch to them. When there is a perfect half-moon in the sky the buffalogres will slaughter all the animals they have captured, and anything the scavagors have given them. If a scavagor was found to have eaten its catch instead of offering the meat to the buffalogres, then there would be fresh scavagor on the menu at the next feast. The buffalogres devour everything, including the bones, then throw some scraps to the scavagors as a reward.'

Hugo was horrified. 'So these buffalogres will eat my uncle at the next Half-moon Feast?'

Pigasus nodded. 'I'm sorry.'

'When is the next half-moon?'

'The night after next,' said Savage quietly.

Hugo jumped up. 'That means we still have two days to rescue him,' he said eagerly. 'We can wait until the buffalogres are all asleep and sneak into the forest and—'

'NO!' Snowdon's loud roar swallowed up Hugo's voice. Hugo stared at him, his mouth hanging open. Snowdon spoke again, but this time in a softer tone. 'We are not going into Tanglefoot Forest. Within the forest's boundary live the most dangerous creatures imaginable. Entry into the forest would mean certain death to anyone crazy enough to try it. And even if somehow we managed to get past the flesh-eating water slugs and the giant vampire beetles and the poisonous three-headed snakes without being eaten alive, we would have no chance of escaping the savage clutches of the buffalogres.'

'But I have to try,' said Hugo. 'What's so scary about these creatures anyway?'

'The buffalogres are the most vicious, repugnant and downright evil creatures ever put on the earth. They are this tall,' Snowdon stretched his arms high above his head, 'and weigh five times as much as me. They have gnarled horns and pink eyes and can outrun most animals. When they hunt they give off the stench of rotten eggs, but if you are close enough to smell them then you are too close to escape.' Snowdon bowed his head towards Hugo and said, 'I'm sorry about your uncle, Hugo. But nobody in their right mind would dare to go into that forest.'

'Prince Erebus would have,' said Delphina, standing as tall as she could.

Snowdon stooped so that his snout was inches from her face. He was trembling with anger, but his voice was steady. 'The prince is gone,' he growled. 'We lost him the night we lost the Silver Acorn.'

With that he lumbered off into the woods, his bright

fur rippling as he crashed through some bushes and into the night.

There was an awkward silence around the campfire. Nobody seemed to know quite what to say.

'Don't worry about him,' said Delphina at last. 'He's not always like that.'

'No,' piped up Savage. 'Sometimes he can be in a *really* bad mood.'

Hugo sat down on a log and pulled his knees into his chest.

'Well, it must be time for dessert,' said Pigasus brightly. He bounded over to a nearby tree and stood on his hind legs, leaning against the trunk. As he shook the tree, fruit fell from its branches, pattering on the ground like fat raindrops. Soon he returned to the campfire with a small pile of berries in his arms. He placed a trotterful in Hugo's lap.

'These are jamberries,' he said. 'They're a bit fresh for my liking, but they're still pretty tasty. The best bit is crunching through the pip. Try one.'

Hugo sadly popped a berry in his mouth. The flesh was sweet, but the pip was about the size of a marble and Hugo couldn't crunch it, no matter how hard he tried. So he rolled the pip around in his mouth for a while and slipped it into his hand when Pigasus wasn't looking.

'You never know,' Delphina said eventually. 'Maybe Snowdon will see things differently in the morning.'

'Maybe,' said Hugo. 'I'm not giving up hope yet. My father taught me better than that.' He smiled bravely and looked around at the strange animals gathered by the fire. 'You're all so different,' he said. 'How did you all come to be here – on this little island?'

'I'll have you know this little island used to be a huge continent, millions of years ago,' said Pigasus.

'When the sea levels started rising, our ancestors were all forced to the higher ground,' said Savage. 'The island you see today is just the tip of the continent.'

'So the sea squeezed you all together?' said Hugo.

'You could say that,' said Delphina. 'We might all look different, but we all get along.'

Savage yawned, stretching his tiny paws into the air. 'I'm going to get my head down for the night,' he said. 'Goodnight, Hugo. Sleep tight. Don't let the flesh-eating water slugs bite.' He scuttled across the mossy ground and disappeared into a tiny hole in a tree stump.

'I'm going to head back to the river,' said Delphina. 'I'll see you tomorrow.'

When she had gone Pigasus explained that Delphina was a merphin so she had to sleep in the river.

'But you can sleep by the fire with me, old chap,' Pigasus said. 'I'm exhausted and you must be too.'

Hugo was worn out, but he was still holding three

jamberry pips he'd hidden from Pigasus. He quickly scraped a shallow hollow in the earth with his heel while Pigasus was making himself comfortable in a pile of leaves. He covered the pips with loose earth and put his satchel on top to hide the little mound he'd made. Then he took one of the blankets from his bag and joined Pigasus on the leafy mattress. As he stared up at the stars Hugo wondered and wondered.

Where was his Uncle Walter, and was he safe? Who was Prince Erebus, and what had happened to him? And what in the world was the Silver Acorn?

Chapter 18

When Hugo opened his eyes he saw two dribbling nostrils looking right back at him. For a moment he was thrilled that he hadn't only dreamed about making friends with a talking flying pig. Then he remembered that his uncle was missing and his heart felt like a rock in his chest.

Pigasus was still asleep when Delphina came to see Hugo, her skin wet and shiny from her night in the river.

'Hi, Hugo. How did you sleep?' she asked.

'Like a log,' he said. 'You?'

'More like a frog.'

'Is there any chance you could show me around Shelter Point?' asked Hugo, keen to get his bearings and begin piecing together his mental map of this strange island.

'Of course. Follow me.'

Delphina led him through a leafy passageway and up a steep earth bank. They had to hold on to tree roots to keep their footing. As they climbed she explained that she could manage on dry land for a few hours, but she couldn't survive much longer without going underwater to breathe. When she turned her head Hugo noticed the gills on the side of her neck for the first time.

At the top of the bank the ground continued to rise but less steeply, and it was soon covered in lush grass. After a while they reached the brow of a round hill that had incredible views of Shelter Point. The land stuck out into the sea like a green arm reaching for the sky.

'It's so peaceful,' said Hugo.

Delphina nodded. 'If only it would stay that way.'

'You don't sound very hopeful.'

'I'm not.' Delphina smiled sadly. 'Shelter Point has been our home for many years and it's always been wonderfully tranquil. But two nights ago a buffalogre found its way through the tunnel. Luckily Snowdon chased it away before it could take anyone. He's pretending that's the end of the matter, but I know he's just trying to keep everyone calm. When they find a source of food, the buffalogres don't waste any time before they hunt it down.'

'Why don't you move to another part of the island?' asked Hugo.

'Shelter Point is the only part of the island the buffalogres haven't already ravaged,' said Delphina. 'There is nowhere else to hide. And next time it won't come alone. We'd be easy meat for a pack of hungry buffalogres.'

Neither spoke for a long while.

'Can I ask a question?' said Hugo at last. 'How did the other human betray you, and what happened to Prince Erebus, and what is the Silver Acorn?'

'You're cheating – that's three questions!' said Delphina. 'But I think I can answer them all with one story.'

Once upon a time someone called Erebus lived on the island. He was tall and strong, a brave warrior who did his best to protect his friends from danger. But he was also a gentle soul who wanted nothing more than peace on the island.

Erebus knew that his only hope of creating true peace was to find the Silver Acorn. According to legend, somewhere within Tanglefoot Forest could be found the Tree of Hope: a mighty oak with a single silver acorn on its branches. It was said that if you held the Silver Acorn, your heart's most cherished wish would come true.

Erebus went into the forest alone and for three weeks he searched high and low for the acorn, fighting off buffalo-ogres, flesh-eating slugs and all sorts of poisonous creatures. No one had ever survived more than a day or two in the forest without being eaten, but somehow Erebus kept going until at last he discovered the Tree of Hope. He picked the Silver Acorn and tied it round his neck.

Instantly Erebus's dream of peace came true – every dangerous creature was instantly tamed. The giant slugs slurped their way quietly into the river to feed on algae while the dark, tangled foliage of the forest sprouted bright flowers of the most amazing pinks and oranges. Even the vicious buffalogres retreated to the hillsides to graze on fresh grass.

Erebus was hailed as a hero and crowned a prince in recognition of his courage. Everyone on the island lived happily ever after . . . for a few years.

Then one night a stranger came to the island. He said his name was Pedro and that he was an explorer from a place called Amazonia. Prince Erebus showed him around the island and let him sleep in Shelter Point. Over dinner Pedro asked Erebus about the silver charm round his neck. The prince trusted Pedro so he told him about the power of the Silver Acorn.

Later that night Pedro sneaked into the prince's hut and stole the acorn from round his neck while he slept. Pedro made his escape, heading for the cover of Tanglefoot Forest. What Pedro hadn't realized was that as soon as the acorn was out of the prince's possession the peace on the island would come to an end. The buffalogres came down from the hillsides, each with the scent of blood in its nostril. After years spent feeding on nothing but grass they were ravenous and were soon on Pedro's trail.

Erebus was woken by the buffalogres' hunting calls screeching through the night. He immediately realized what had happened and went after Pedro as fast as he could. Somehow Pedro made it through Tanglefoot Forest alive, but the buffalogres caught up with him on the beach at Violet Cove. When Erebus arrived on the clifftop, Pedro was surrounded.

Pedro pleaded with the prince to help him. He said that he had hidden the Silver Acorn on the island, and that he would take Erebus to it if he protected him from the buffalogres. Erebus did his best to fight off the beasts, but after years of exile in the mountains they were more savage than ever. Pedro became part of the buffalogres' Half-moon Feast, and the prince was lucky to escape alive. The Silver Acorn has never been found and the shadow of danger has darkened the island ever since.

Chapter 19

When Delphina had finished telling her story Hugo realized that his mouth was hanging open. A small puddle of saliva had collected on his shirt.

'That's incredible!' he said, wiping his chin. 'Prince Erebus sounds like a real hero.'

'He is. I mean, he was,' said Delphina.

'Is he dead?'

Delphina nodded. 'He survived a few days. But in the end he died from his battle wounds.'

'Why are the buffalogres so evil?'

'Well, if we go even further back in time, legend says that the buffalogres used to lie dormant way beneath the ground – imprisoned deep within a labyrinth of caves and tunnels. The threshold to this evil underworld was said to be a cave in the mountains. The animals of the island were forbidden to go near the cave for fear of disturbing the monsters that existed below.

'In those days the island was peaceful and the animals foraged and fished for their food. Over time a society grew, led by Fuji, a distant ancestor of Prince Erebus. The animals learned to communicate and settled on the edge of Tanglefoot Forest.

'But one day some water slugs ventured blindly to the mouth of the cave, enchanted by the smell coming from within the mountain. They followed the scent to the heart of the labyrinth.'

'What happened?' Hugo whispered.

'The slugs woke the sleeping buffalogres,' said Delphina. 'There was a massacre. Most of the slugs were devoured instantly or roasted on the fires of hell. Only a few escaped by following their own slime trails back through the labyrinth and into fresh air. Unfortunately they were followed by the buffalogres and the other evil beasts that lived underground – the vampire beetles and three-headed snakes.

'It was a half-moon that night. That's why the buffalogres have a feast every half-moon. To celebrate the night the water slugs freed them from their tomb.'

'And – apart from Erebus's reign of peace – the island has lived in fear ever since?'

Delphina nodded. 'When the sun came up the monsters from the underworld couldn't bear the light. The snakes and beetles fled to the darkness of Tanglefoot Forest. The buffalogres remained in the open, hunting for their feast, but the sunlight left them almost blind.'

'And what about the scavagors?' asked Hugo. 'Why do they serve the buffalogres?'

'Because they are weak,' said Delphina. 'When the buffalogres first escaped it seemed like no animal would survive the night. Fuji fought like a true warrior, but he could only protect so many. The scavagors cut their losses and sided with the buffalogres to save their own skins.'

Hugo could see that Delphina was upset. He said nothing for a long time, thinking about the buffalogres and Pedro and the Silver Acorn until his head was spinning.

'Why did Pedro hide the Silver Acorn on the island?' he said at last. 'Why didn't he just keep it in his pocket or something?'

Delphina shrugged. 'Nobody knows,' she said. 'It's a mystery. Just like the mystery of where that piece of wood got to.'

'What piece of wood?' said Hugo.

'Didn't I mention that?' said Delphina. 'When Pedro was asking Prince Erebus to protect him he showed him a small piece of wood. He said he'd written the acorn's location on it. Before he died Erebus returned to the beach. He spent his last days searching for it but it never showed up. The sea washed it away, I suppose.'

Hugo grabbed her arm, his eyes suddenly bright with excitement. 'Or maybe the sea washed it into a narrow crevice in the cliff face where it has been preserved ever since.'

'Er, maybe,' said Delphina, frowning.

Hugo jumped up and started running downhill. 'Come on.'

'Why are you so excited?' said Delphina, sprinting to catch up.

'I think I've seen the clue. I know where the piece of wood is.'

'Where?'

Hugo stopped and gave Delphina a big smile. 'It's in my satchel.'

Chapter 20

Hugo and Delphina ran all the way back to the clearing, charging past Snowdon, who was going out to collect firewood.

'Where have you been?' he barked.

'Hugo thinks he's found the clue left by Pedro,' Delphina called over her shoulder.

Pigasus was still sleeping by the embers of the fire when they sprinted into the clearing, skidding to a halt on the dewy grass. They were both out of breath, but couldn't help laughing with excitement.

'Where's your satchel?' Delphina gasped.

'It's here somewhere,' said Hugo, scanning the ground.

Pigasus snorted loudly and sat up. He was squinting to shield his eyes from the sun, and one of his ears was sticking up where he'd been sleeping on it.

'What on earth is all the fuss about?' he complained. 'How dare you wake me up so hideously early?'

Hugo looked up. Through the leafy canopy he could see the sun directly overhead. 'But, Pigasus, it's nearly midday,' he said.

'Is it?' said Pigasus. 'Good heavens! I'd better get up.

I'll have to hurry if I'm going to have time for my breakfast before lunchtime.'

'We can't have you skipping any meals,' said Delphina, 'or you'll waste away.'

'My point exactly,' said Pigasus, scratching his huge round belly. 'Are there any of those jamberries left?'

Suddenly Hugo remembered. Last night he'd buried three jamberry pips in the ground and covered the mound of earth with his bag. He bounded over to the tree stump he'd been using as a stool and just behind it was his satchel. As he picked it up Hugo noticed three bright green shoots growing out of the earth, each about four inches long, with a tiny pink bud at the tip. They must have grown from the jamberry pips overnight, he realized with a shock.

Delphina's excited squeals distracted him from wondering any further. 'Is it there?' she said. 'Have you still got it?'

'Got what?' said Pigasus, through a mouthful of cold eel and patata.

'He says he's got the clue to where the Silver Acorn is hidden,' said a quiet voice in the bushes. Snowdon emerged, carrying a few small trees in his strong arms. He let them fall to the ground and began stripping the branches off one, ready to be chopped into logs. 'Well, Hugo?' he asked. 'Have you got it or not?'

Hugo opened the flap of his satchel and looked

inside. Lying among the blankets was the small piece of driftwood he'd found in the crevice of the cliff. He turned it over to look at the strange symbols etched into it, then held it out for the others to see.

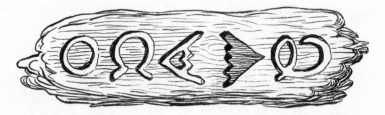

Snowdon's fur bristled.

Delphina held her webbed hands to her mouth.

Pigasus gasped, then started choking. Snowdon gave him a couple of hard whacks on his back, and a piece of eel shot out of his mouth like a bullet. The morsel missed Hugo by inches and stuck to a tree behind him.

'Is that really the clue?' said Delphina.

'Where did you find it?' asked Snowdon.

'In a cave on the beach,' said Hugo. 'Near where Pigasus rescued me yesterday.'

'Then this could actually be it,' said Snowdon.

He took the piece of wood from Hugo, moved away and studied it. It looked like a twig in his huge hairy paws. Delphina and Pigasus crowded round him to get a closer look. Even Savage emerged from his tree stump to see what was causing the commotion. Eager to secure the best vantage point, he scampered up Snowdon's body and along his arm. Clambering precariously on to the piece of wood he examined each symbol in turn, his whiskers twitching with curiosity.

For what seemed like ages the four of them discussed the clue among themselves. Hugo tried desperately to hear what they were saying. Even though he sneaked a few steps closer to the huddle, he could only make out the odd snippet of their whispered conversation.

Eventually the little group broke up and Snowdon approached Hugo, who pretended he hadn't been listening by staring closely at a leaf and whistling.

'Well, Hugo,' said Snowdon, 'we're all agreed that this is the clue to the location of the Silver Acorn.'

Hugo jumped from foot to foot with excitement. 'So . . . where is it?' he asked.

Snowdon knelt down and put a huge paw on Hugo's shoulder. 'We don't know. None of us has ever seen any writing like this before. We think it's some sort of foreign script.'

Hugo's excitement withered like a balloon punctured on a thorn bush. His chin dropped on to his chest and he let his satchel slide to the ground.

'But that piece of wood is all we've got,' he said, his voice breaking with despair. 'It's our only hope of finding the Silver Acorn and bringing peace to this island. It's my only hope of finding Uncle Walter. It has to mean *something*.'

'You have to face facts, Hugo,' said Snowdon. 'The Silver Acorn is lost forever . . . and so is your uncle.'

Delphina gave Snowdon a sharp look. 'The only thing that's lost forever is your courage,' she said. 'Hugo, I have to take a swim now. Why don't you come with me and meet Kramer? We can ask him if he understands the clue.'

'He won't know what it means,' muttered Snowdon.

'If I didn't know you better, Snowdon, I'd think you were pleased that we don't understand what the clue means,' snapped Delphina. 'I think you're relieved you don't have to venture into the forest. I think you're a big scaredy-snout.'

Snowdon began to disagree, but Delphina, Savage and Hugo had already left.

Chapter 21

It was cool and still by the river. The clear water drifted slowly over round pebbles, easing from left to right as it meandered through the trees.

Delphina said she'd go and find Kramer while Hugo and Savage waited on the bank. They watched her wade in until the river lapped gently around her hips. Then she dived under the water and with one swift kick of her webbed feet she glided out of sight. A single circular ripple remained.

'Is Kramer another merphin?' asked Hugo.

'You'll have to wait and see,' laughed Savage, his whiskers tickling Hugo's ear.

But Hugo wasn't in the mood for another riddle. The more he thought about the task ahead, the more desperate he felt. He clenched his hands round his pendant to stop them shaking.

'I can't just sit here and do nothing,' Hugo said.

'Well, what would you be doing if Uncle Walter were here now?' asked Savage.

'We'd be making a map of this fantastic island,' said Hugo, smiling at the thought.

'Why don't you give it a go then?' suggested Savage. 'It might make you feel better.'

Hugo took his notebook and some charcoal out of his satchel and started sketching. From memory he drew the coastline, and he etched in the fog bank. He drew a small ship to denote the position where *El Tonto Perdido* was anchored and he marked in the cave on Violet Cove where he had spent the night. He used shading to indicate the cliff face and detailed two birds with rats' heads where the scavagors had snatched Uncle Walter.

Then he outlined the curved finger of Shelter Point and marked in the stream with its lazy curves. He sketched the jagged ridge as a narrow ellipse and drew a dotted line to denote the tunnel. Then he drew the trees, as he had seen them from above, using a different symbol for each species. Some had sharp, spiky leaves, so he drew them with jagged edges. Others were rounder so he drew them like clouds.

'You're right,' said Hugo. 'Drawing this map makes me feel calmer – as if Uncle Walter wasn't so far away after all.'

Eventually Delphina emerged from the river. For a moment Hugo thought she was alone, but then he saw another creature slip out of the water behind her. He gasped.

Swaggering lazily up the bank towards them was a two-headed crocodile. Its back was rough with scales and its mouths were curled into two smarmy smiles. Its pointed tail dragged along the ground, swinging from side to side with each step.

'Hugo,' said Delphina, 'I'd like you to meet Kramer.'

Hugo tried to swallow. 'H-h-hello, Kramer.'

'Don't be afraid,' said one of the heads. 'We won't eat you.'

'No. I've just had breakfast,' said the other head. 'So I'm not hungry . . . YET.'

'He's joking,' said the first head.

'Of course I'm joking,' said the other head. 'I'm actually starving!'

Hugo managed a small laugh.

'Delphina has told me all about the mysterious piece of wood,' said the first head. 'Can I see it? I'm usually quite good at solving puzzles when I put my heads together.'

Hugo handed the clue to Kramer. First one head, then the other scrutinized it, like a jeweller valuing a diamond.

'Well?' said Hugo. 'Do you know what it means?'

'Give me a moment,' said one head as water dripped from the tips of both alligatory noses. 'Yes, don't rush me,' said the other head, grinning. 'You wouldn't want me to make any *snap* decisions now, would you?'

'Of course not,' said Hugo. 'Take jaw time.'

Eventually, though, Kramer had to admit defeat. He

had no idea what the clue meant. Hugo, Savage and Delphina tried to hide their disappointment.

'At least you put your minds to it,' said Delphina.

Kramer noticed Hugo's notebook and asked what he was drawing. Hugo showed him the map, explaining how it represented the island as if seen from above. Kramer, who had never seen a map before, was fascinated. He studied it carefully, nodding his heads as he began to understand how it depicted the island's territory.

'And what does this bit down here mean?' asked Kramer, pointing to the bottom left-hand corner with one of his sharp claws.

'Oh, that's the key,' said Hugo. 'That's where the mapmaker explains all the symbols on the map.'

He showed how the spiky circles were the trees with sharp leaves, and the cloud shapes were the trees with the rounder leaves.

'That's very clever,' said Kramer, shaking his heads in wonder. 'And what's this shape down here?'

'That's a short segment of the river,' said Hugo. 'It's just one curve – just an example.'

'Hmm,' said Kramer thoughtfully. 'It's funny.'

'What's funny?' said Hugo and Delphina together.

'It's probably just a coincidence,' said one of Kramer's heads, 'but that symbol showing a single curve of the river is very similar to the second letter of the clue.'

His other head nodded and said, 'I was just thinking the same thing.'

Hugo looked at the key on his map, then at the strange symbols on the piece of wood. His heart raced and he felt hope swelling in his lungs. Suddenly he understood! The clue didn't spell a word, and it wasn't a foreign alphabet. The symbols weren't even letters. They were pictures.

'This isn't a clue at all,' Hugo gasped. 'It's some kind of map.'

CHapter 22

Hugo sprinted back to show Pigasus and Snowdon what he had discovered. Delphina and Kramer followed close behind, while Savage struggled valiantly to catch up. Gasping for breath, the tiny mouse scampered as fast as his little legs could carry him, his ears flapping horizontally behind him, like pink flags.

When they ran into Snowdon, on his way down to the river to fish for eels, Hugo, Delphina and both Kramer's heads all spoke at once – talking excitedly over each other so that none of them could be heard clearly. Savage arrived and slumped at the foot of a sapling, his lungs heaving under his soft fur.

Snowdon held his club up in the air. 'Silence,' he ordered. Hugo and Delphina hushed up immediately, but Kramer kept talking, his heads arguing with each other.

'I saw the map first.'

'Yes, but I said it was like the clue before you did.'

'I was thinking it though.'

'Were not.'

'Was so.'

'I said SILENCE,' roared Snowdon. This time both sets of jaws snapped shut immediately.

'Hugo,' continued Snowdon more quietly, 'tell me what you are all so excited about.'

Hugo showed him the map he had drawn and explained how the key worked. He pointed out that the bend in the river was just like the second symbol of the clue left by Pedro.

'This piece of wood is some sort of map. I think it describes the landscape where the Silver Acorn is hidden. Pedro must have drawn it so that he could come back for the acorn. The second symbol is a river and I think the last symbol is supposed to be the acorn. If we can identify the other symbols, we can definitely find the Silver Acorn and save my uncle – but we have to hurry. The half-moon is tomorrow night.'

Snowdon seemed decidedly unimpressed. 'And what about the other symbols?' he said. 'What does the first one represent?'

Delphina shrugged. Kramer looked confused and shook his heads. Hugo frowned and studied the circular shape.

'You don't have much hope of finding the acorn if you don't even understand the first symbol on your map,' said Snowdon with a sneer. 'Are you going to wander around the whole island trying to find an unknown bend in an unknown river?'

'Don't you know what the shape might mean?' asked Delphina.

'I have absolutely no idea,' said Snowdon immediately.

'I'm surprised at you, Snowdon,' said Pigasus, emerging from a clump of trees where he had been collecting fruit. 'It's one thing to give up on the Silver Acorn yourself, but it's quite another to obstruct others from achieving something you daren't undertake.'

'What's that supposed to mean?' snarled Snowdon.

'You know as well as I do that Tanglefoot Forest grows in the shape of a perfect circle,' said Pigasus. 'And I'm sure you know that's what the first symbol of Pedro's map depicts.'

'Of course!' said Hugo, remembering the bird's eye view he'd had of the forest when he'd flown across the island on Pigasus's back.

'It hadn't occurred to me,' said Snowdon unconvincingly. 'Besides, the area within the forest is huge. It could take you days to find that particular bend in the river – by which time you'll have been eaten alive.'

'We'll find Noah,' said Pigasus. 'If anyone can decode this map, it's him.'

'Noah Tall?' scoffed Snowdon. 'Good luck! Even if he could solve the puzzle of Pedro's map, he won't give you any straight answers. He talks in the most elaborate riddles and you'll come away more confused than you were to begin with.'

Hugo desperately wanted to ask who this Noah Tall was, but judged (correctly) that now wasn't the right time to ask.

'Too many of us have already died trying to recover that acorn,' said Snowdon. 'You'll be lucky just to survive Tanglefoot Forest.'

'We have to try at least,' said Hugo. 'The buffalogres will come back to Shelter Point soon. If we're going to protect ourselves, then someone has to follow that map into Tanglefoot Forest. Yes, we might not survive, but if we do nothing, we'll all die for sure. My father taught me never to give up until the game is over – and this game isn't over yet.' Hugo took a deep breath. 'I'm going to try and save my uncle – with or without help from any of you. Now . . . who's with me?'

Silence cloaked them for a moment.

Then suddenly Savage sprang up and darted across to a large cactus. 'I'm with you, Hugo,' he declared, plucking a spine from the plant. 'With my strength and your determination we'll teach those monsters not to meddle with us.' Up on his haunches, Savage swiped and stabbed with the cactus spine as if it was a sword. 'Take that, and that! Those buffalogres won't know what's hit them.'

'Thank you, Savage,' said Hugo. He was touched by

his mouse-friend's loyalty, but he had been hoping that someone else might join him too. Someone bigger.

'Ha!' sneered Snowdon. 'What chance do you two stand?'

Hugo puffed out his chest and looked up at Snowdon. 'A pawn and a knight can defeat a whole army.'

'I'm the knight, by the way,' said Savage, thrusting with his cactus spine. Then he muttered to no one in particular, 'I'm not even entirely sure what a pawn is.'

'Come on, then, Sir Savage. Let's go,' said Hugo, looping the strap of his satchel over his head. Savage darted up Hugo's clothes and on to his shoulder.

'Now hang on just a minute, Hugo,' said Pigasus. 'As you may have guessed, I'm not the world's greatest fighter. I'm about as far from being a hero as it's possible to get, in fact – I'm much too fond of eating and sleeping to be any use battling buffalogres . . .'

Pigasus paused to push a peach into his mouth – then he continued with sudden verve. 'However . . . I'll be darned if I'm going to wait for the buffalogres to come and snatch me from my bed.'

Hugo smiled appreciatively as Pigasus went on, 'Obviously Delphina and Kramer can't go because we don't know how long it'll be before we find a river for them to breathe in.'

'I'll stay and guard the tunnel,' said Kramer.

143

'I'll come some of the way,' offered Delphina. 'I don't need water as often as Kramer.'

Hugo turned to Snowdon. 'What about you, Snowdon?' he asked. 'Are you in or out?'

Snowdon slung his net over his shoulder. He studied the small group gathered before him, and sighed. 'I'm out.'

CHApter 23

Hugo, Pigasus and Delphina walked in single file towards Tanglefoot Forest, with Savage riding high on Hugo's shoulder. The air was hot and damp, the sun fierce overhead. They crossed a meadow of incredible turquoise grass and passed bushes with golden leaves shaped like hands. Orange bell-shaped flowers dwarfed them, and giant red daffodils seemed to nod in greeting as they passed. When they stopped for a rest Hugo added these plants to his map.

As well as his notebook he had packed a few peaches and patatas in his satchel, which was slung across his body. He was carrying a large stick for protection. Pigasus had 'borrowed' a bow and some arrows that he thought Snowdon wouldn't miss. Even though he'd never fired the weapon in his life, he felt safer with it. As protection, Delphina had tied a slipknot in Hugo's measuring rope, which was coiled up and slung over her shoulder, and Savage was armed with his cactus spine. None of them wanted to admit to being nervous, so they joked about their adventure.

'Who's afraid of flesh-eating water slugs anyway?' scoffed Savage.

'And what's so scary about vampire beetles?' said Hugo.

'Yeah,' laughed Pigasus manically. 'So what if they are twice as big as you, with teeth like hooked daggers?'

Hugo swallowed nervously.

'They only come out at night though,' said Delphina quickly. 'We'll be out of the forest by sunset.'

'Exactly,' said Pigasus with relief. 'Nothing at all to be afraid of.'

Reassured, they strode bravely onwards.

A little later Hugo said, 'So who is this Noah Tall, then?'

Pigasus explained that Noah Tall was the Oracle – the oldest and wisest creature on the island. Legend said he lived within the forest but had the power to make himself disappear and reappear anywhere he wished. He used this gift to evade danger, and unwanted visitors, so he was incredibly hard to find. It was rumoured that he only helped those with right on their side.

'We just have to hope that he wants to be found,' said Pigasus.

The closer they got to the forest, the more anxious the group became. After a couple of hours they were all so nervous that they were marching in silence . . . until Pigasus spun round and called out, 'Who's there?'

There was no reply.

'I'm sure I heard footsteps behind me,' said Pigasus.

'Everything's going to be fine,' said Savage. 'I'll protect you.'

'Er . . . thanks, old chap. I feel so much safer now, knowing that my entire well-being rests in your tiny paws.'

As they continued to tease each other a figure watched them from about thirty yards away. Crouched down behind a thick bush with long spiral leaves, it watched them march out of sight. Then it followed, keeping its distance.

When he reached the brow of a grassy hillock Hugo stopped suddenly. Savage wasn't holding on and went flying forward off his shoulder, clutching at the air with his claws. Hugo reacted quickly, just managing to grab Savage's tail as he fell.

'Sorry about that,' said Hugo. 'Are you all right?'

'Never better,' snapped Savage, swinging upside down like a furry pendulum.

'Why have we stopped?' said Delphina.

'Look down there,' said Hugo.

At the bottom of the hill, just a short distance away, was the edge of Tanglefoot Forest.

The trees were immensely tall with intertwined, gnarled branches, like ancient giants linking arms to form a barricade. Their thick leafy coats hissed spitefully in the breeze, and their trunks overlapped, leaving no space for any light to pass in or out. Beneath its emerald canopy, Tanglefoot Forest was as black as night.

The group stood in awed silence.

After a moment Hugo spoke. 'I was thinking about those vampire beetles. I've just realized something.'

'What's that?' said Delphina.

'Well, you said they only come out at night. The thing is, by the looks of it, it's always night in Tanglefoot Forest.'

'Don't worry about a few vampire beetles,' said Savage, lunging at an imaginary fiend with his cactus spike.

'I can just about hear the beetles quaking in their shells already,' said Pigasus.

Hugo and Delphina looked at each other uncertainly.

'There isn't any better way into the forest,' said Delphina. 'We don't really have much choice.'

'Pigasus, couldn't you just fly me over the forest?' suggested Hugo brightly.

'If only I could, my dear boy,' sighed Pigasus. 'My poor petite wings are still exhausted from our little adventure yesterday. I can barely lift them, never mind flap them.'

Hugo nodded. 'Then into the forest we go.'

Hugo led the way, ducking his head under low-hanging branches. For safety – and to conserve energy for the fight ahead – Savage had opted to ride in his pocket. It was cold and damp under the cover of the trees, and so dark that Hugo couldn't even see his own feet as they squelched in the muddy earth. He turned to check that the others were following.

'Pigasus, Delphina, are you there?' he called, making his eyes as wide as he could to try to see in the gloom.

Then he felt something pat his chest a couple of times. He stepped back but it patted him again, then clutched his arm. Hugo jumped with terror.

'Help! Help! It's got me,' he screamed, thrashing his arms about. 'Come quickly. Pigasus, Delphina, help me! It's going to suck my blood!'

Hugo heard a familiar voice right next to his ear. 'Do calm down, dear boy,' said Pigasus softly. 'It's only me that's got you, and I assure you I'm not about to suck anything – least of all your blood.'

It was hard work making any headway with the branches grabbing their clothes and fur and the mud sucking hard at their feet. They clambered over twisted roots and ducked under low branches, forcing their way through the dense foliage – until Hugo was faced with a thick tree trunk, as wide as he was tall, with rough, knobbly bark that made deep gouges down the tree. Hugo was studying the bark with interest when in the middle of the trunk two bright blue eyes opened. They were perfectly round, with wide pupils, and they blinked curiously at him.

Frozen with fear, Hugo stared back. Then, to his amazement, the tree spoke to him.

'You should never have come into the forest,' it hissed. 'Death awaits all those who enter.'

'I-I-I don't want to c-c-cause trouble,' stammered Hugo.

'You will be punished for your foolishness,' said the tree. 'Tanglefoot Forest will be your grave.'

Trembling like the leaves around him, Hugo gripped his stick and waited for the tree to attack. Just then Delphina appeared, closely followed by Pigasus.

'That tree just threatened to kill me,' Hugo said, nodding at the knobbly trunk. 'It said I was going to die in the forest.'

'Oh dear, I think you're still a bit shaken up, Hugo,' said Delphina anxiously. 'Trees don't speak.'

'You're quite right, Delphina,' said Pigasus, smiling. 'Trees don't speak. But owls do.'

As he spoke a sleek, snowy owl stepped out of a hollow in the tree trunk and peered down at them. Its plump white breast was speckled with deep purple tufts and its round eyes seemed to glow like two blue planets. With its wings folded neatly behind its back it had an air of quiet authority.

'It's a sentinowl of the forest,' said Delphina with relief. 'He's just being friendly.'

'Friendly?' exclaimed Hugo. 'It said the forest would be my grave.'

'It was only warning you of the danger that lies ahead – trying to scare you away for your own good.'

Pigasus raised a trotter and thanked the owl for its concern. He assured it that they knew about the dangers within the forest, but that they were determined to search for the Silver Acorn.

'Then I wish you all good luck,' whispered the owl, before sidling back into the hollow.

'Did you really think the tree was going to attack you?' said Savage, clambering out of Hugo's pocket. 'I could tell all along that it *wooden* hurt a fly.'

'It did look scary to start with,' insisted Hugo. 'But I suppose you could say its bark was worse than its bite.'

Delphina sighed wearily. 'I think that's quite enough tree jokes.'

'She's right,' said Pigasus sternly. 'Let's just *leaf* it there. I think we should concentrate on which *root* to follow.'

Hidden by the jungle of trees, another pair of eyes watched them very closely indeed as they made their way deeper into the forest.

Chapter 24

For hours the world seemed to stand still. With no sun the gang had no idea what time of day it was, and it was too dark to judge how much of the forest was behind them – nor how much lay ahead.

They were all tired but Delphina was suffering the most. There was just enough moisture in the damp air for her to breathe, but she was feeling weak and in need of a long swim to replenish her lungs.

'I know things seem tough,' said Hugo as they ploughed along, 'but at least we haven't met any vampire beetles.'

'That's true,' said Savage. Then: 'What's that noise?'

'I can't hear anything,' said Pigasus. 'I think your preposterous ears are deceiv—'

A buzzing sound filled the forest, cutting him off. It quickly grew louder until Hugo had to cover his ears. Something black and shiny flashed past his face. Delphina screamed as it zoomed back the other way, knocking Pigasus to the ground. Then to Hugo's great relief the buzzing stopped. He slowly took his hands away from his ears and turned to see the most hideous sight of his life, just a few yards away and staring right at him.

Hugo ran his eyes over the monster from the ground up, studying its ugliness in silent awe. Its antennae twitching, it folded its delicate wings away under its armoured shell. It had six angular legs, each in three segments, clad in the same glossy armour that protected its wings. About the size and shape of an upturned rowing boat, its body had two shell segments that overlapped at the neck like hunched shoulders. Its head was a flat teardrop-shape like a helmet, split at the front into two savagely hooked fangs.

The insect's head panned slowly from side to side, searching for its prey. Its fangs moved like lethal pincers, clicking together loudly in anticipation of a bloody feast.

'So I'm guessing this is a vampire beetle?' breathed Hugo.

'Don't move,' whispered Pigasus, who was lying in an awkward heap on the floor. 'It's completely blind but its antennae will pick up the slightest movement.'

Hugo was about to nod to show he understood, but he stopped himself. The harder he tried to stay still, the more aware he became of his body's movements. Could this monster sense his stomach moving in and out beneath his loose shirt as he tried to contain his breathing? Would it home in on his eyes moving around in their sockets, or his heart thrashing wildly in his chest, or even Savage twitching nervously in his pocket?

Delphina was finding it just as difficult to remain motionless. She had ducked when the beetle had flashed past her head and was now frozen in an awkward semi-crouched position. She was already weak from water starvation, and now her legs were in agony from holding the squat.

Without warning she fainted, collapsing to the floor with a weary groan.

The beetle's head snapped round in Delphina's direction. It scuttled over to her, its legs moving in a rippling motion like fingers drumming on a table. As the beetle passed within inches of his face Hugo felt the hairs on his arms stand up – but he didn't move. Instead he watched helplessly as the giant insect loomed over the unconscious Delphina.

It picked her up with its two front legs and reared up on to its spindly haunches. She hung limply from the monster's grasp like an old rag doll. The giant beetle tilted its head back and opened its fangs wide.

'We have to do something,' whispered Savage from Hugo's pocket.

Hugo nodded once.

Without pausing to think he ran up behind the beetle and, with all his might, hammered his stick down on to the insect's back.

'Take that, and that!' he screamed.

But the beetle was completely untroubled by Hugo's

onslaught. The giant insect merely turned its head towards him, wiggling its antennae furiously as if to pinpoint his exact position. Then it turned back to Delphina and opened its fangs hungrily once more.

'Pigasus!' ordered Hugo. 'Use your bow and arrow.'

Pigasus scrambled to a kneeling position and drew an arrow from the quiver on his back. With a straight arm he held the bow out and fed the arrow into it. Holding the string of the bow in the cleft of his trotter he drew it back to his cheek, and like an expert archer closed one eye and stared along the length of the arrow. When he was sure he had the vampire beetle in his sights he let the arrow fly.

The arrow slashed through the air at deadly speed. Unfortunately it missed the beetle by at least ten yards and disappeared into the forest, where it pierced a distant tree trunk with a twang.

'What was that supposed to be?' hissed Hugo.

'I'm sorry,' said Pigasus, shrugging. 'I've never fired this thing before.'

The beetle's fangs were now closing round Delphina's neck. Hugo had to do something fast. Gripping his stick like a spear, he crept up behind the beetle, aimed the pointed end of his stick at one of the insect's legs and stabbed it, right between the segments of armour.

The vampire beetle screamed and flailed its limbs

wildly. Dropping Delphina to the ground, it spun round to face Hugo. It lashed out with a leg, knocking the stick from his grasp. As Hugo desperately scrabbled to retreat, he tripped on the uneven ground and fell on his bottom. The beetle towered over him, its fangs thrashing away angrily. Hugo tried to scramble backwards but felt his head bang against a thick tree trunk and realized he had nowhere to hide.

Savage sprang from Hugo's pocket and scampered towards the beetle, stabbing at one of its legs with his cactus spine.

'Take that!'

The beetle didn't flinch.

Hugo heard another arrow ping from Pigasus's bow. He felt a surge of hope, until it became clear that the arrow was once again completely off target.

The vampire beetle snatched Hugo up. Spiky hairs over the tips of its legs gripped his clothes like glue. Hugo stared into the gaping hole between the insect's sabre-like fangs. Then the vampire beetle jerked violently. It dropped Hugo to the ground and staggered back a couple of paces. Hugo watched with confusion as the beetle teetered back and forth – reminding him of Oliver Muddle drunkenly trying to get his balance. A thick dark liquid started spraying from the beetle's mouth, spattering into the air as it coughed. For a few more seconds it tottered, then came crashing to the ground – toppling on to its front like a felled tree.

Hugo stood in silence and watched the beetle for any sign of movement. After a moment Savage scampered over to inspect the fallen beast. Tentatively he circled it once, keeping his distance from its outstretched limbs – then began to leap up and down, throwing his paws up and kicking his legs out to one side.

'I take it that little jig means he won't be bugging us any more?' asked Hugo.

'I think he finally got the point,' laughed Savage.

Hugo stared at the monster lying lifeless before him. Embedded in its back, piercing the narrowest of gaps between the segments of its body armour, was an arrow. Hugo looked up in amazement to congratulate Pigasus on his incredible shot.

Beyond the body of the vampire beetle knelt Pigasus, who looked even more amazed than Hugo. But Pigasus wasn't holding the bow. Kneeling next to him, with the bow held at arm's length as its string hummed softly, was Snowdon.

Chapter 25

Hugo ran over to Snowdon. He wanted to hug him, but he just looked up into his face and smiled.

'Thank you. You saved my life.'

Snowdon patted Hugo's head with his huge paw. 'Well, you saved Delphina's life, and Pigasus saved mine. So that makes us all even.'

Snowdon crouched down to check on Delphina. She was conscious now, but still very weak.

'Is she going to be all right?' asked Hugo.

'She'll be fine. We just need to get her to some water.'

'I'm still confused,' said Savage. 'How did Pigasus save your life, Snowdon?'

'I was following you through the forest. I wanted to make sure you would be all right. When the vampire beetle turned up I was about to attack it. Then the biggest three-headed snake I've ever seen dropped on to me. I managed to chop off two of its heads with my broadsword but I wasn't fast enough to get the third one. It was about to sink its poisonous teeth into me when Pigasus came to the rescue.'

'Did I?' said Pigasus with a start. 'I mean, yes, I did.'

'How exactly?' asked Savage, looking at Pigasus incredulously.

'I . . . er . . . well, I don't like to brag.'

Snowdon let out a deep chuckle. 'That second arrow Pigasus fired at the vampire beetle missed it by a mile. But it did hit the snake right between the eyes – killed it instantly.'

'What an amazing stroke of luck,' giggled Hugo.

'What do you mean, "luck"?' said Pigasus indignantly. 'I knew Snowdon was following us. I saw him just before we came into the forest. I was going to kill the beetle, but then I saw Snowdon struggling with that hideous snake in the distance.'

'Really?' said Savage. 'You must have incredible eyesight to have seen all that way in this darkness.'

'I can assure you my eyesight is second to none,' said Pigasus. 'It was a tough call, but I had to make an instant decision. I knew Snowdon was in more immediate danger than Hugo so I killed the snake.

'So why didn't you kill the beetle with your first arrow?' said Savage. 'Instead of firing it into the forest way over there?'

'Well . . . um . . . that's a very good question,' stuttered Pigasus. 'I . . . er . . . Well, you see . . .'

'I think you were probably just finding your range, weren't you?' suggested Hugo.

'That's it, exactly,' said Pigasus. 'A good marksman always has to set his sights with a practice shot.'

A moan from Delphina reminded them that they needed to find water. Snowdon said he could hear a stream nearby and suggested they all rest there for a while. He gathered Delphina up in his arms and led the way through the forest, his stubby tail wagging from side to side as he walked.

'Why did you change your mind about coming with us?' asked Hugo, following behind.

'Two reasons,' said Snowdon. 'I'll tell you while we rest.'

The small campfire glowed deep orange, but its light was swallowed up quickly by the blackness of the forest. It looked like a fiery planet in the night sky. Hugo, Savage and Pigasus sat close to the fire while Snowdon patrolled around them, ready to start his explanations. Delphina lay in the stream, letting the fresh water flow through her gills.

'Firstly, I thought you might need this,' said Snowdon. From a cloth sack he produced a sword in a scabbard and handed it to Hugo. Hugo gripped the handle and drew the blade. He hefted the sword, feeling its weight, and chopped it through the air as if fighting an invisible opponent.

'It's beautiful,' said Hugo, admiring the intricate design of the sword's hilt. 'Thank you.'

'It belonged to my father,' said Snowdon. 'He was as big as me so it was just a dagger to him, but it's a good-sized sword for you.'

'Have you got a weapon for me?' said Pigasus.

'Well, you're such a skilful archer I thought you should keep my bow and arrows.'

'Of course. Nothing will be safe when I'm firing these arrows.'

'Not even any of us,' remarked Savage under his breath.

Something suddenly occurred to Hugo. 'Do we know what Pedro wished for once he had the acorn?' he said.

'You don't make a wish when you have the acorn,' said Snowdon gravely. 'It's not a magic lamp. The Silver Acorn looks deep into your soul and grants whatever desire you hold most dear. You may think you want one thing, but your heart might crave something else – something you have never admitted even to yourself. To this day no one knows which selfish desire of Pedro's was granted by the acorn.'

Pigasus interrupted the ensuing silence. 'What's the other reason?'

'Sorry?'

'You said there were two reasons you came to help us. You thought Hugo should have the sword, and . . . ?'

'Ah yes,' said Snowdon. 'When you left Shelter Point you said that your plan was to find Noah Tall and ask him about the map.'

The others nodded.

'Well, I might be able to help you there,' said Snowdon. 'Years ago when I was just a cub and this island was still at peace, my father and I met Noah Tall. His advice was confusing and senseless and led us nowhere.'

'How does that help us now?' said Hugo.

'I went to his house,' Snowdon smiled. 'I know where Noah Tall lives.'

Snowdon insisted the others should sleep for a few hours while he kept watch over them. Hugo closed his eyes tightly but he couldn't relax. He sighed.

'What's the matter, Hugo?' asked Savage, curling up close to his face.

'I keep wondering what my heart's deepest desire is,' Hugo replied. 'I mean, I'm pretty sure I want peace on the island more than anything because that would guarantee Uncle Walter's safety. But I have always dreamed of being captain of my own ship one day, or a world-famous mapmaker. What if either of those desires is stronger? What if I'm too selfish to save my uncle?'

Savage's whiskers twitched. 'I think that if you really

were that selfish you wouldn't be lying here awake worrying about it,' he said.

'Maybe.'

'As soon as we find the Silver Acorn you and your uncle will be back on that ship and on your way home.'

A thought occurred to Hugo and he suddenly felt helpless. 'That's if the ship is still waiting for us,' he said. 'Maybe they think we're never coming back. Maybe they've already sailed for home.'

CHapter 26

'They'll never be back,' said Hawkeye, casting his eye across the wall of fog fifty yards from *El Tonto Perdido*.

'I don't see no point in hanging around here no longer,' said Rusty Cleaver, dishing out their dinner. 'That boy and the old man will have been boiled alive by natives by now.'

'Or worse,' said Rockford.

None of the sailors could think what might be worse than being boiled alive by natives, but they didn't want to argue with their colossal, muscle-bound shipmate. They all nodded.

'What's on the menu tonight, Rusty?' asked Swipe. 'Not pickled beef and biscuits again?'

'No. I'm trying out a new recipe,' said Rusty. 'Biscuits and pickled beef.'

Oliver Muddle tapped a biscuit on the deck and a white maggot dropped out. He picked up the maggot and popped it wriggling into his mouth. Then he threw the biscuit overboard. 'What's the admiral having for his tea?'

'I told him it's beef stew and dumplings,' said Rusty with a sly grin.

'What is it really?' asked Hawkeye.

'Pickled beef and biscuits.'

'The man's an idiot. What shall we say to him about moving on then?' said Oliver Muddle.

Bandit and Swipe exchanged worried glances.

'If we sail any further west, we'll surely fall off the edge of the world,' said Bandit.

'The old man said the world was round,' said Muddle.

'Then how come the people at the bottom don't fall off?' smirked Swipe.

'He said it's because the world is spinning really fast,' said Muddle.

Bandit drained his tankard of ale. 'Maybe that's why I feel so dizzy all the time,' he laughed.

The sailors hadn't heard Rupert come out of his cabin. He was standing behind them on the main deck. 'That's what I like to hear,' he said. 'The sound of my crew relaxing and enjoying themselves. I like a bit of banter myself, as it happens. What are you all nattering about?'

The sailors looked down at the deck. Hawkeye rolled his eye. No one spoke.

'You can't beat some good old-fashioned seafaring chit-chat,' Rupert said. 'Carry on, men. Pretend I'm not here.'

Somebody coughed.

'How about a song?' suggested the admiral. 'I bet you chaps know some shanties that could turn my hair blue!'

Silence.

In the distance, something squawked.

'Well, it's lovely to chat,' said Rupert. 'Really, really . . . er . . . lovely. By the way, Seaman Cleaver, the stew tonight was a little dry. And the dumplings were really quite crunchy. Stale even. I do hope standards aren't going to be allowed to slip.'

'No, Admiral,' muttered Rusty. 'Sorry, Admiral.'

As Admiral Lilywhite turned to leave, Rockford dug Oliver Muddle in the ribs. Muddle groaned and Rupert turned back. 'Seaman Muddle,' he said, 'was there something you wanted to say?'

Oliver Muddle looked around at the crew. They glared meaningfully back.

'Well, s-sir, me and the men, we been t-talking,' he stammered. 'And we've concluded that the mapmaker and his boy ain't coming back to this ship. They've been gone two nights now. If we go further west we'll fall off the earth, so we feel it's time to turn back and head for home.'

Rupert looked at the group of men sitting in a circle before him. He sensed an air of unease – a whiff of dissent. He would have to choose his words carefully if he was to regain his crew's unstinting support.

'Men, you have no idea what you're talking about,' he said. A ripple of protest stirred the sailors. Rupert squirmed. 'What I mean is that you don't understand – we don't understand. The mysteries of this world are beyond the comprehension of simple men. And there are no men on this earth more simple than you.'

Rupert paused. The sailors looked at him in silence. A few mouths were hanging open. Taking this to be a sign of respect, he continued: 'We are a team and we are all equal . . . except for me because I'm in charge, obviously. We will not leave before the mapmaker and his apprentice come back with enough coconuts and information to make me famous. Now, if you'll excuse me, I'm going to lie down in my cabin.'

Rusty ground his teeth as he watched Rupert leave.

'If they're not back by nightfall tomorrow, we're heading for home,' he scowled. 'Whether Admiral I'm-in-charge Lilywhite likes it or not.'

Chapter 27

Hugo was woken by Snowdon rocking him gently by the shoulder.

'Time to get moving.'

They made much quicker progress with Snowdon leading the way through the forest. He used his huge broadsword to chop through the dense undergrowth, slashing through thick branches as if they were twigs.

As they walked Hugo remembered the story Delphina had told him about Prince Erebus. He tried to imagine him fighting his way through Tanglefoot Forest alone, searching for the Silver Acorn.

'What sort of creature was Erebus?' he asked after a while.

'Well, he died before I was born,' said Pigasus, 'but they say he was a tremendous leader whose bravery was matched only by his intelligence – so I think we all know what that means.'

'You're not suggesting Erebus was a flutterhog?' Delphina laughed.

'Modesty forbids me from saying another word on the subject.'

'Rubbish!' protested Savage, jumping on to Hugo's

head excitedly. 'Erebus wasn't warty and breathless; he was handsome and powerful – just like me.'

'Erebus a chattermouse?' snorted Pigasus. 'I've never heard anything so ridiculous in all my life. He was a mighty warrior, not a tiny little rodent.'

'Maybe he was a mighty warrior *for his size*,' retorted Savage.

'Do you know, Snowdon,' asked Delphina, 'you're probably the only one old enough to have met Erebus.'

'What difference does it make?' growled Snowdon, angrily chopping at the undergrowth. 'Erebus is gone and no one on this island could ever replace him. That's all there is to say.'

Everyone trudged on in silence.

After about an hour they noticed the world getting brighter, with shadows and textures appearing out of the darkness. Soon they were looking at rolling meadows covered in flowers of every possible colour. They were finally out of Tanglefoot Forest!

Squinting in the bright sunlight, Hugo marvelled at the kaleidoscope of flowers scattered all around like confetti. Overhead the sky was clear powder blue. The sun was already some way above the horizon, which made Hugo feel suddenly anxious.

'It must be at least nine o'clock already,' he said. 'We have to hurry. Tonight's the Half-moon Feast.'

'How far to Noah Tall's house?' said Pigasus.

'If my memory serves me right,' said Snowdon, his nose twitching in the air as he surveyed the scenery, 'Noah Tall lives just over there.'

The others looked in the direction Snowdon was pointing. All they could see was a carpet of grass and petals rising and falling gently into the distance. Hugo glanced at Savage, who was sitting up on his shoulder.

Savage shrugged in bemusement. 'Maybe Snowdon's fight with the three-headed snake has sent him crazy,' he whispered.

'I know,' said Hugo. 'Perhaps his brain was starved of oxygen when the snake tried to strangle him.'

'I hate to be the one to spoil this moment of great elation,' said Pigasus, 'but there is no house *over there*, Snowdon. All there is *over there* is grass, flowers and a rotten old tree stump.'

'Thank you, Pigasus, for your excellent observational skills,' said Snowdon. He strode over to the tree stump, closely followed by his companions, knelt down and knocked on it five times with the hilt of his sword.

They waited. Nothing happened.

'Maybe he's moved,' said Pigasus. 'You know, sold up and bought the upturned bucket in the city he's always dreamed of.'

Just then there was a loud pop and a small cloud of pink glitter appeared above the tree stump. As the cloud dissipated it slowly revealed a troll-like figure – the smallest man Hugo had ever seen. He was no more than twelve inches tall, and about the same across. His eyes peered out from the wiry hair that covered his rotund body and his droopy nose hung down like a warty sausage. His oddly large hands and feet seemed to protrude straight from his body and he wore shoes that had been carved out of wood.

'Yes?' he said impatiently.

'*You're* Noah Tall?' asked Pigasus.

'Who were you expecting, the King of Spain?'

'No, we were looking for you,' said Hugo quickly. 'We just expected you to be a little bit . . . you know . . .'

'Taller?' said Noah Tall.

Hugo nodded apologetically.

'I see. Because my name is Tall you thought I would be tall. How very literal of you,' said Noah. He sighed wearily. 'Are you also under the impression that a dandelion is a particularly fashionable wild cat? Or that a sausage dog is in fact made out of pork? I can only imagine your disappointment when you saw your very first clothes horse. Hello, Snowdon – haven't you grown up?'

Snowdon grunted.

'So what brings you back after such a long time?' said Noah.

'This wasn't my idea,' said Snowdon.

'He's joking,' laughed Savage. 'He's a big fan of yours. Huge.'

Delphina explained that they thought they had found Pedro's clue to the Silver Acorn's location. She told Noah they believed the clue to be some sort of map that would guide them to it. Hugo produced the piece of wood from his satchel and showed it to him.

'Before I study this I must warn you all that I am forbidden from giving any straight answers,' said Noah Tall. 'That is rule number one in the *Pocket-size Oracle Rule Book*. I am at liberty only to guide you. My wisdom is a gift, but I would be doing no one any favours if I just gave you information willy-nilly. You must find the solutions for yourselves. Work as a team and you will succeed. Remember: you must learn to think for yourselves if you are to be worthy of finding your prize.'

Snowdon snorted. The others nodded their consent to the terms.

'Well, I suppose we'd better do this officially,' continued Noah. 'The Overseer of Oracles says that all wisdom must be passed on in rhyme. So here goes.' He cleared his throat.

'Learn to think as you go along
And your chance of success will grow strong.
When I'm not there to guide or teach
The Silver Acorn will be in your reach.

Knowledge earned is wisdom learned,
But knowledge given is soon forgotten.'

Noah Tall shifted awkwardly for a second. 'I know, I know . . . that last bit doesn't rhyme,' he said apologetically. 'Just because I'm wise doesn't mean I'm good at poetry. And I challenge any of you to come up with a good rhyme for "given".'

The others agreed tactfully that 'given' was a very difficult word to rhyme with.

'I'll be back in a jiffy,' said Noah Tall, disappearing in a puff of sparkly dust.

'Where's he gone?' said Delphina.

Suddenly there was another glittery puff and Noah reappeared, adjusting a dusty old cocked hat on his head.

'Sorry about that,' he said. 'Just had to put my thinking cap on. Now let's have a look at this map.'

The piece of wood was too big for Noah Tall to hold, so Hugo held it for him. He studied the symbols carefully.

Suddenly Noah's wooden shoes started knocking together loudly.

'Oh, you know where the map is leading, do you?' he said to his shoes. 'What a pair of clever clogs.'

By now Hugo had seen so many magical things on the island that he realized he wasn't at all surprised that Noah Tall's shoes were able to decipher the map – or even that they could talk.

'What are they saying?' he asked.

'Patience!' said Noah Tall. 'Only when you have solved one clue can my thinking hat and clever clogs help you decipher the next. You must start by finding this horseshoe-shaped bend in the river.'

'We know that much already,' said Pigasus. 'Is there any chance you could tell us something we haven't worked out for ourselves?'

Noah thought for a moment then said,

> 'Which way should you travel?
> Well, that's up to you.
> Start Out Under The Hills,
> That's my initial clue,
> And what do you know?
> It even rhymes too.'

There was another puff of spangly dust and Noah Tall was gone.

'Is that it?' said Pigasus. 'Is that all he's going to tell us? It doesn't even make sense. How can you start out under a hill? You can't get under a hill anyway – you can only get over it.'

'Start out under the hills?' repeated Delphina. 'What I don't understand is that he emphasized that it was his first clue, but then he didn't give us another one.'

'Let's all take some time to think about it,' said Hugo. 'It has to mean something.'

'Or it could be total piffle,' muttered Snowdon.

'As you're here you might as well help us,' said Delphina sharply.

They all tried to figure out the puzzle in their own ways. Every now and then Pigasus would snort with frustration or Snowdon would shake his head. Delphina sat quietly with her chin resting on one hand. Hugo took out his notebook and wrote the clue down so he could study it more carefully. Savage clung to Hugo's sleeve, looking from the notebook to Hugo's face and back again.

'I can't concentrate with you staring at me,' said Hugo.

'Sorry,' said Savage, his whiskers twitching. 'Just pretend I'm not here.'

Time passed. No one spoke.

Hugo could almost feel the sun panning across the sky.

Eventually Snowdon snarled with frustration. 'This is a waste of time,' he said. 'This riddle is impossible. We've all tried our best, but now it's time to head back to Shelter Point. None of us will survive if we're out here when the half-moon rises.'

'No!' cried Hugo. Desperately he looked to Delphina and Pigasus for support.

'Snowdon is right,' said Delphina reluctantly. 'If we can't make sense of Pedro's map, then we're lost.'

'I hate to admit it, old chap,' said Pigasus, placing a trotter on Hugo's shoulder, 'but I think Snowdon has a point. Let's go home.'

Hugo shrugged Pigasus off, his blood pumping. He could feel his head throbbing. He felt helpless and hopeless. 'Maybe you're right,' he mumbled. Then he heard a voice in his ear.

'Never give up,' whispered Savage. 'You can do this. What would your father tell you?'

Pigasus, Snowdon and Delphina were already making their way back to Tanglefoot Forest. Hugo clutched the wooden chess piece hanging round his neck. He closed his eyes and thought about his father and the moment he had given him the pendant and explained its inscription. He opened his eyes and read the words carved around its base: Honest, Undaunted, Gallant, Optimistic.

Hugo held his breath for a second. 'That's it!'

He whooped and threw his hands up with delight, tossing Savage off his cuff and high into the air. Savage performed a complete somersault and landed on top of Hugo's head, clutching at strands of hair to stop himself slipping off backwards.

Hugo plucked his little friend from his hair and placed him back on his shoulder.

'I take it you have some promising news?' asked Savage.

'I've solved it!' Hugo yelled.

Hearing the commotion, Pigasus, Snowdon and Delphina hurried back to hear Hugo's solution.

Hugo explained. '"Start out under the hills" isn't Noah Tall's first clue. He said it was his *initial* clue.' He couldn't help enjoying the look of confusion on his friends' faces. He went on, 'So what are the initials of "Start Out Under The Hills"?'

'S, O, U, T, H,' said Pigasus, still looking bewildered.

'Obviously spelling isn't his strong point,' Savage muttered.

'It spells "south",' exclaimed Delphina.

'Exactly,' said Hugo. 'Noah Tall thinks we'll find the river bend if we head south.'

'At last!' said Pigasus. 'I was wondering how long it would take you lot to catch on. I mean, I'd solved the riddle immediately, but I didn't want to show off – especially as I'd already saved everyone once in the forest.'

'Of course you did,' said Savage. 'I don't know where we'd be without you.'

'Follow me, then,' said Pigasus, and he started marching away with big confident strides. It was a minute before he turned round and saw that no one was following him.

'What are you all waiting for?' he demanded.

'Well, it's just that we're supposed to be going south,' said Hugo. 'And you are most definitely heading north.'

'Just testing,' said Pigasus, scampering back to join the others.

As they headed south, Savage's whiskers tickled Hugo's ear. 'Well done,' he whispered. 'You did it.'

'No,' said Hugo. 'We did it.'

Chapter 28

Hugo was feeling more positive. The hot sun was warming his bones and he was suddenly very grateful for his new friends. Savage was still teasing Pigasus about setting off in the wrong direction. Up ahead, Delphina was scurrying to keep up with Snowdon's lumbering strides.

Then something happened that reminded them all just how dangerous their mission really was.

They were wandering across a meadow when Snowdon dived to the ground. 'Get down!' he whispered urgently. Pigasus, Hugo and Delphina immediately threw themselves to the ground. Savage scurried into Hugo's waistcoat pocket.

Off to their right was a small cluster of trees. Snowdon crawled over to the copse on his elbows, then beckoned for the others to follow. They all scrambled behind the trees as quickly as they could. Keeping his head low, Snowdon pointed and put a finger to his lips.

About thirty yards away, loping from left to right across their path, were six huge, hairy, hideous beasts. They looked incredibly powerful, their thick shoulders and muscular haunches clad in coarse, woolly hair. Their heads hung low as if weighed down by their three twisted horns, and they each snorted hungrily through their single nostril. Hugo was pretty certain he knew what these creatures were. Then a light breeze blew the stench of rotten eggs their way and he was sure.

Snowdon mouthed the word 'Buff-al-o-gres'.

A sudden gust of wind blew an extra whiff of their strange odour right up Hugo's nose and into the back of his throat. Before he could stop himself he coughed. The buffalogres stopped immediately and looked over to the trees where he was hiding.

'Don't move,' whispered Snowdon. 'Stay exactly where you are.'

One of the buffalogres stepped closer to the cluster of trees. Twigs and cones snapped loudly under its immense weight. Hugo stayed frozen. The monster took a couple of strides in his direction. Now, just a few feet away, its ugly pink eyes were swivelling wildly in their sockets low down on either side of its wide head. As it snorted and snarled Hugo could see ferocious teeth lining its powerful jaws.

'OK, so he may not be the prettiest animal on the island,' whispered Savage, 'but I'm sure he's charming once you get to know him.'

The buffalogre took another step forward. Now it was actually standing astride Hugo, who peered at the thick tail thrashing from side to side like an angry snake. The stench of rotten eggs was becoming unbearable: Hugo could feel it reaching down his windpipe and twisting his stomach. His eyes were watering and his nose was running and he felt like he was going to be sick.

A thick dollop of saliva dropped from the buffal-ogre's mouth and oozed down the side of Hugo's face. Disgusted, he could feel himself retching. He tried one last time to contain his cough, but it was no good.

'HHEEUUGH!'

For once, luck was on his side. At exactly that moment one of the other monsters let out a hideous ear-piercing screech that completely drowned out Hugo's cough.

Two more buffalogres in the field screeched. Then Hugo saw why they were all so excited. A young mammoth had trotted out of a nearby grove, unaware that it was exposing itself to these vicious monsters. The small, shaggy-haired elephant froze when it heard the screeching. Its ears fanned out and its trunk reared up. Then it saw the buffalogres and fled.

The baby mammoth moved surprisingly quickly. Its head bobbed desperately as it tried to reach the safety of some trees. But it was no match for the speed and agility of the buffalogres. Within a few seconds they had cornered their prey. The mammoth was bigger than the buffalogres and it took two of them to wrestle it to the ground. Exhausted and terrified, it lay still as the buffalogres dragged it out of sight.

Appalled, Snowdon started to follow, but Delphina put a hand on his arm to stop him.

'Don't go now,' she said. 'It would be almost impossible to fight off all those buffalogres. We need you to help us find the Silver Acorn. If we find it before the half-moon rises tonight, that young mammoth will be freed along with Hugo's uncle.'

'Where are they taking that poor creature?' said Hugo.

'The buffalogres live in a labyrinth of caves hidden deep inside the mountains,' said Pigasus. 'They keep their prey in dungeons there until it's time for the feast. That's where your uncle must be.'

'Even if we do find the acorn, how will we find the caves?' said Hugo.

'We'll find them,' said Snowdon sternly. 'I'll make sure of that.'

CHapter 29

Rusty Cleaver went to the admiral's cabin to collect his lunch plate and offer him dessert. At the carved oak door he wiped his hands on his bloodstained apron and grasped the ornate brass knocker. He was just about to bang on the door when he heard talking coming from inside the cabin. Curious, he gently replaced the knocker and leaned forward, pressing his ear against the cold wood.

Rusty recognized Admiral Lilywhite's voice immediately. Although it was muffled he could just make out what was being said.

'You should be proud of yourself, sailor,' enthused Rupert. 'You have set an excellent example to the crew and they all admire you greatly. Soon the mapmaker and the boy will be back and our mission will be accomplished – all thanks to you. Without your invaluable skill and expertise this expedition would certainly have failed.'

Desperate to discover the identity of the admiral's hero, Rusty crouched down to peer through the keyhole. Much to his annoyance, though, the key was in the lock, blocking his view. He couldn't see that Admiral

Lilywhite was actually alone in his quarters, talking to himself in the mirror.

'Oi, Rusty! What are you playing at?' hissed Bandit, who happened to be passing on his way to his shift at the ship's wheel.

Rusty spun round and held a finger to his lips. 'The admiral's talking to someone in there,' he whispered. 'He's saying that our voyage would have failed without him.'

Silently Bandit pulled a shocked face. Then he joined Rusty, pressing his ear to the door.

Rupert was now admiring himself from different angles.

'To be honest it's a wonder we ever made it out of the harbour with this crew!' he said, shaking his head gently so as not to disturb his hair. 'Heaven knows where we'd have ended up if you hadn't told Seaman Muddle that the sun sets in the west. Muddle by name and muddle by nature, if you ask me.'

Rusty and Bandit covered their mouths to stifle their sniggers.

'And as for Bandit,' Rupert continued, 'he's about as much use on a ship as a one-armed juggler.'

Rusty shoved Bandit playfully. Bandit glowered back.

'Mind you, that Rusty Cleaver is no better.' Rupert

raised one eyebrow at his reflection. 'The only recipe he seems to have perfected is the recipe for disaster.'

This time it was Bandit who was laughing. He shoved Rusty back.

'In fact, they've all been utterly useless except you,' Rupert continued, giving himself a toothy grin. 'That's why, when we return to England, you will take all the credit for this momentous discovery, and the rest of the crew will get nothing. You'll be rich and famous and they'll be forgotten.'

'Right, that's it,' said a furious Rusty. 'Let's go and tell Muddle what our loyal admiral is planning.'

As they turned to leave, the hilt of Bandit's sword bumped against the cabin door. A moment later the door opened.

'Who's out there?' Rupert called.

'It's only me and Bandit,' said Rusty as the pair of them jumped to attention. 'We've just come to . . . er . . . collect your plates.'

'Wait here.' Rupert disappeared into his quarters, leaving the door ajar.

Bandit eased the door open a little more, and he and Rusty scanned the room in the hope of spotting the traitor within.

'Are you two all right?' said Rupert when he returned and handed the crockery over. 'Have you lost something?'

'We ain't lost nothing,' said Rusty.

'And we didn't hear you talking to nobody neither,' added Bandit for good measure.

'That's because there's nobody here,' Rupert retorted quickly. 'And I wasn't even talking to anybody. Least of all myself.'

The three men eyed each other suspiciously for a moment. Then Rusty spoke: 'Come on, then, Bandit. Let's go and wash up all these dishes.'

'Wash up? I thought we were going to tell Mudd— Oh yeah, right. Let's go and wash up.'

Rusty and Bandit turned to leave.

'By the way, are there any desserts on the menu today, Seaman Cleaver?' Rupert called. 'I rather fancy a small slice of sponge and maybe some pie.'

Rusty turned round. 'Certainly, sir. And would you care for another drink, Admiral?'

'No, thank you,' said Rupert. 'Just desserts for me.'

'Aye aye, Admiral.' Rusty grinned broadly. 'Just desserts coming right up.'

CHapter 30

The five companions continued heading south, their mood sombre after the mammoth hunt. As they trudged along in silence Hugo couldn't help imagining Uncle Walter imprisoned inside the monsters' labyrinth, awaiting the same fate as the poor elephant.

After some time the grass became steadily longer, and before they knew it they were forcing their way through thick reeds that were taller than everyone except Snowdon.

When Snowdon started walking more quickly through the rushes Hugo suspected he could see something hopeful. And, sure enough, after a few more steps they stumbled out of the long grass on to a pebbly river bank.

The shape of the river was exactly like the shape of the second symbol on Pedro's map!

Ridges of foam and whirlpools formed on the river's surface, then disappeared as the water coursed downstream. Instead of flowing straight, the river turned sharply, almost flowing back on itself. Then it made a wide horseshoe shape, almost returning to the beginning of its diversion before continuing its original path across the island.

Hugo felt a trill of excitement. Then he noticed something he thought might mean trouble. Lying on the peninsula that formed the centre of the horseshoe were two fat, shiny slugs, their slimy brown skin mottled with mustardy yellow spots.

'What are *they*?' said Hugo, his nose wrinkling with disgust.

'Water slugs,' said Snowdon.

'Flesh-eating water slugs, to be precise,' added Pigasus.

'They look gross,' said Hugo. 'They'd never attack us though, would they? I mean they're so fat and, well, sluggish.'

'Looks can be deceiving,' warned Snowdon. 'They may look lazy, but these slugs are lethal hunters. They have an incredible sense of smell, they can crawl faster than any man can run and their slime is the strongest acid on the island. Once it has cornered you, a slug will crawl on top of you, dissolving you into gunge, and then absorb your body through its skin.'

190

Hugo was still pondering that particular method of dying when Delphina spotted something else. Beyond the slugs basking in the sun, on the opposite riverbank, there was a small circular rowing boat. It was made out of segments of leather sewn together. Lying in the boat were two wooden oars.

'Is that how Pedro got across the river?' said Hugo.

Snowdon shook his head. 'Pedro had no boat. But when he stole the Silver Acorn this river had almost no current. He would have been able to swim across easily. Since then this island has suffered ferocious rainstorms, which have swollen the river's volume and caused it to flow more vigorously.'

'But how did Pedro get past the slugs?' said Pigasus.

'The same way he managed to survive Tanglefoot Forest, I suppose,' said Snowdon. 'With sheer luck.'

Delphina frowned. 'If that boat wasn't left there by Pedro, who did leave it?'

As Hugo peered across the river at the boat he noticed something sparkling in the bright sunshine.

'Look! The boat is covered in glittery dust,' he said. 'I think our pocket-sized guide is trying to help us across the river.'

'Maybe I was wrong about Noah,' said Snowdon, surprised.

'I don't wish to appear ungrateful,' said Pigasus grumpily, 'but it would have been a darn sight more helpful if he'd left it *this* side of the river. However, I have an idea that might just save the day.'

'Well, don't keep us all in suspense,' urged Savage.

Pigasus cleared his throat before presenting his plan. 'I shall fly across the river and row downstream a short distance to avoid the water slugs. Then I'll head back across to collect you lot, and modestly accept your words of gratitude and admiration.'

'Do you think your wings are rested yet?' asked Hugo.

'There's only one way to find out.'

Pigasus began to flap his wings. He flapped and he flapped but nothing happened. He took a deep breath and tried again. He flapped until his face was purple, but his trotters never left the ground. Eventually he stopped flapping and his little wings hung limply from his back like two soggy rags.

'It's no use,' he said. 'I can't do it. I hope you don't think less of me.'

'Pigasus, old friend,' said Savage, 'it would be very difficult for me to think any less of you.'

'I must still be exhausted from flying all the way back from Violet Cove with young Hugo on my back.'

'And me,' said Savage.

'Of course,' said Pigasus. 'It must have been your considerable extra bulk that wore me out.'

'Never mind – I'll go!' said Delphina. 'I can swim faster than a warty water slug any day.'

'What if they catch you?' said Hugo.

'They won't,' said Delphina defiantly, and before anyone could stop her she darted out of the reeds and headed down the steep shingled bank. Just as she got to the water's edge she stopped. A circular ripple had appeared on the surface of the water in front of her. The circle grew bigger, then the water parted as a squidgy lump emerged from the river. It started shuffling up the riverbank at an incredible rate.

As the killer slug reared up before her Delphina leaped high into the air, somersaulting over its head. Landing silently behind it, she slipped Hugo's rope from her shoulder. While the slug was still struggling to locate her Delphina swung the loop of rope over her head. As she twirled it faster the noose at the end grew into a wide, flat circle. By this time the poisonous slug had sniffed her out and its body bent double as it turned to smother her, two tiny nostrils on the top of its head twitching hungrily.

With a flick of her wrist Delphina flung the lasso at her opponent. The rope hoop quivered only slightly as it sailed through the air and dropped round the killer slug's amorphous body. With one sharp tug Delphina yanked the noose tight, squeezing a narrow waist into the monster's bulbous physique.

'Well done, Delphina!' cheered Pigasus.

'That slug's *bound* to stay put now,' laughed Savage.

'It certainly doesn't look too well,' said Hugo. 'Maybe it's feeling a bit ropey.'

The fat creature writhed in protest as Delphina leaped high over it again, landing next to a large boulder round which she lashed the loose end of the rope. Quickly she darted back down the bank, keeping just out of reach of the tethered slug. As Delphina escaped, the angry slug tried to chase after her, but was jerked rudely on to its back.

'Ha! Serves you right, you revolting slime monster!'

She ran to the river's edge and was just about to dive in when two more slugs emerged from the river and slithered swiftly towards her.

Delphina turned and scrambled up the bank towards the safety of the reeds. The two slugs that had been sleeping in the sunshine noticed the commotion and joined the chase. All four slugs were gaining on her and suddenly she didn't stand a chance.

Then Snowdon came crashing out of the long grass. He charged down the riverbank, roaring and wielding his sword above his head with two paws. Without stopping, he ran straight past Delphina, who was struggling up the bank in the opposite direction.

In a flash he sliced his sword right through the nearest slug, chopping its top clean off as if it was a soft-boiled egg. The decapitated slug collapsed to the ground, oozing horrible green gloop over the pebbles.

Snowdon turned and pelted along the riverbank. The surviving slugs went after him, their bodies arching and straightening as they shunted along the pebbles, each one leaving a trail of thick slime behind it.

Delphina realized that Snowdon was creating a diversion and turned back towards the river. She dived silently into the water, leaving a single round ripple behind her. With her legs together she arched her body, kicked her webbed feet and darted out of sight.

'Look out, Snowdon!' cried Hugo suddenly.

One slug had caught up with Snowdon as he struggled up a grassy slope. Snowdon turned to fight it off with his sword, but another slug bumped him from the side with its blunt head, sending him to the ground. Snowdon struggled to get up but it bumped him again, knocking him flat. He was surrounded.

'We have to do something,' said Hugo. 'Pigasus, try to think how we can help Snowdon. Pigasus?'

Silence.

'PIGASUS?'

'They've probably smelt us already,' whimpered Pigasus. 'They'll track us down and sit on us and dissolve us with their disgusting slug juices. I bet they're sniffing us out right now.'

'You're not being especially helpful,' said Savage.

Somehow, though, Pigasus's terrified, panicky ramblings had given Hugo a brilliant idea.

Chapter 31

Hugo took off his satchel and hastily delved inside. Nestling in the corner, safely wrapped in a cloth, were the hens' eggs he had taken from Admiral Lilywhite's ship. Their shells were cold and smooth and fitted neatly into the palm of his hand.

'I really don't think this is the best time to be thinking about breakfast,' said Savage.

Ignoring him, Hugo asked Pigasus to pass him two arrows, which he lay down at his feet. Then he took one of the blankets from his satchel and tore off two strips of cloth, each one about three inches wide. He wrapped the eggs in the strips of cloth and tied each one to the shaft of an arrow, just behind its flint-stone point, making a little sling. He handed the arrows back to Pigasus.

'Shoot these at the slugs,' Hugo instructed.

Pigasus took an arrow and fed it proudly into his bow. 'Which slug do you want me to hit?' he asked as he drew back the bow.

'I don't mind.'

'Should I aim for its head or its tail?'

'Either will do,' Hugo said, getting impatient.

Pigasus peered down the length of the arrow, studying his target. He aimed a bit to the left then up a bit and a little bit back to the right. Hugo glanced over at Snowdon. He had been knocked over again and one of the slugs was already half on top of him.

'This is an exceedingly difficult shot to make,' said Pigasus. 'I have to compensate for the slight breeze and the slope of the terrain, not to mention calculating the effect that the weight of the egg will have on the arrow's flight.'

Savage leaped from Hugo's shoulder and landed spreadeagled on Pigasus's snout. 'Oh for heaven's sake, Pigasus!' he snapped. 'Just fire the arrow.'

Pigasus let the arrow fly. It arced through the air – heading way off target – before the weight of the egg tipped it downwards. The arrow landed on the pebbled riverbank about ten yards short of the water slugs.

As the arrow hit the ground the egg bounced on a rock and cracked open. Its raw insides oozed out of the broken shell and crept over the pebbles.

'Oh dear, that wasn't terribly successful,' said Pigasus, shaking his head forlornly.

'Nonsense, that was a cracking shot!' said Hugo. 'Fire the other one – quickly!'

Pigasus did as he was told and the second arrow landed on the other side of the water slugs. As before, the egg cracked open on the stony ground.

'Now what?' asked Pigasus, who couldn't see why Hugo was looking quite so pleased.

'We just have to hope those eggs are rotten,' said Hugo.

The eggs were rotten all right. They were already weeks old when Hugo had taken them from the hens' coop on board *El Tonto Perdido*. After a few days of being warmed at the bottom of Hugo's satchel they were as rotten as rotten can be. Their yolks were hideous yellow-green slime and their awful stench travelled potently in the gentle breeze.

'What an extraordinary smell!' said Pigasus, his snout twitching in the air.

He wasn't the only one to have noticed the whiff. As Hugo had hoped, the smell of rotten eggs meant only one thing to the water slugs – buffalogres!

Abandoning Snowdon immediately, all four fled instinctively for the river. Like a herd of giant walruses they flopped into the water, thrashing their tails about violently. In a storm of froth and spray they swam away downstream, leaving the river foaming behind them.

'The slugs are making a swift egg-sit,' said Savage.

'I always knew they were spineless,' giggled Hugo.

Pigasus smiled triumphantly. 'As soon as the eggs broke they scrambled,' he said.

Hugo and Pigasus ran over and helped Snowdon to his feet. The fur on his legs was matted with slug juice.

He waded into the water to wash it off. The acid hadn't damaged his skin but it had singed his fur. Now the flowing fur on his legs was cropped short, making him look like a giant poodle.

Hugo and the others waited and watched as Delphina fought to manoeuvre the boat back across the ferocious stretch of water. The boat was heavy and awkward, and the powerful current constantly urged her downstream. It was an epic struggle, but eventually Delphina reached the near shore and slumped over the oars.

'Have a seat,' she gasped, barely able to speak. 'Now let's get across this river and find that Silver Acorn, shall we?'

Delphina rested her head on Hugo's shoulder while Snowdon rowed the boat across the fast-flowing river with long powerful strokes. Even with his considerable size and strength he had to battle hard to resist the fierce current, but finally they reached the far side.

'We have to keep moving – but maybe you should stay here and rest, Delphina,' said Snowdon, panting hard as he tethered the boat to a rock.

'But I want to help find the Silver Acorn,' she protested. 'I've come this far – I want to see this thing through to the end.'

'You have helped already,' said Snowdon. 'None of

us could ever have swum across the river. Without you we would never have made it this far.'

'Fine,' said Delphina reluctantly. 'I'll wait here and keep an eye on the boat.'

Hugo rummaged in the bottom of his satchel and offered three more eggs to Delphina.

'Take a couple of these,' he said. 'If those slugs do return, just crack one open. They'll think the buffal-ogres are back and you won't see them for froth.'

Delphina took two of the eggs. 'Thank you, Hugo,' she said, waving them off. 'And good luck, my friends.'

Hugo set off up the riverbank with Savage clinging to his shoulder. Pigasus and Snowdon followed. When Hugo looked back Delphina was already hiding in the long grass.

'I was wondering, Hugo,' said Pigasus as they walked. 'If nobody else wants it, could I have the last egg?'

'Of course,' said Hugo. He handed him the pinky-brown egg. 'Are you worried you might need it to protect yourself from more flesh-eating water slugs?'

'Good heavens, no!' said Pigasus. 'I'm starving, that's all.'

Pigasus tossed the egg into the air and caught it in his mouth. Snorting and snuffling, he crunched up the shell and swallowed its rancid contents. A trickle of slime the colour of snot dribbled down his chin. 'Egg-squisite!' he said.

'Yeuch! That's horrible,' said Hugo. He was holding his nose, but he couldn't help laughing. 'Now you've got buffalogre breath.'

Chapter 32

The grass near the river was tall and thick, but it became shorter the further they walked from the river-bank. Very soon it felt like a velvety lawn under their feet. A narrow gravelly path led off through the meadow.

Hugo studied the next symbol on Pedro's map.

He had no idea what it meant.

'Does anybody have any ideas?' he said.

Savage blinked. 'I was just enjoying the ride.'

'Not a clue, I'm afraid,' said Pigasus.

'Let's have a look around,' suggested Snowdon. They could see open meadows dotted with small clumps of trees and three tall snow-capped mountains in the distance. They could see flowers like oversize blue dandelions and miniature sunflowers, but there was nothing that resembled the symbol on the map.

'Are we lost?' said Hugo.

'Of course not. We know exactly where we are,' said Pigasus cheerily. 'We just don't know where we're going.'

Hugo sat down on a clump of grass and hung his head. 'I'm not much of a mapmaker, am I? I can't even understand a simple key. At this rate, I'll never see Uncle Walter again.'

'I know what will cheer you up,' said Pigasus. 'I'm off to find you some peaches – nice and rotten, just the way you like them.'

Hugo managed a sad smile.

'Don't be downhearted,' whispered Savage. 'You'll find your way. I'm sure of it.'

'Over here. Quickly!' squealed Pigasus, seconds later.

'Probably just needs a hand with his famous peaches,' muttered Snowdon as they rushed over to see what had got Pigasus so excited. Savage gripped Hugo's waistcoat as he ran, his furry little body bucking into the air with each stride.

Pigasus was now a short distance away from where they had stopped. The path crossed another one at right angles, making a crossroads. Lying next to the junction was a square post with four wooden signs nailed to the top. There was a square hole in the ground that the signpost would fit into exactly.

The signpost pointed in four different directions, each one represented by a single symbol. Snowdon picked up the post and held it upright. Spinning it in his paw, he examined each sign in turn.

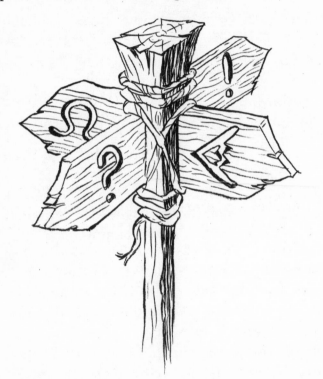

'I found this too,' said Pigasus. He pointed to a flat rock

lying near the crossroads. On the surface of the rock someone had etched a message. Hugo read it out.

> 'Steer clear of danger
> And avoid the unknown.
> Take the right path
> And you'll soon be home.
> PS That counts as a rhyme in my book.'

He smiled. 'It's another clue from Noah Tall.'

'I've got it!' said Pigasus. 'He says we should "take the *right* path". So we turn right, right?'

The others weren't convinced.

'Maybe he just means we must choose the *correct* path,' said Hugo.

'Surely all we have to do is put the signpost back in the ground and follow the path marked by this symbol,' said Snowdon. He pointed to the sign marked:

'But how do we know which way it goes in?' asked Hugo. 'A square peg goes into a square hole four ways.

We could make any sign point to any path, but only one way would be correct. If we got it wrong, we could get horribly lost . . . or worse.'

'First let's work out what each of the symbols means,' suggested Savage.

Hugo thought that ? was supposed to represent 'the unknown' referred to in Noah Tall's poem. The others agreed, and they decided that this meant that | stood for 'danger'. They already knew that ⟨ was what they were trying to find, and the Ω symbol signified the bend in the river where they had fought the water slugs.

'Well, chaps, this is quite a conundrum,' said Pigasus. 'We don't know which path leads to danger, and we haven't a clue which way is the unknown.

Hugo's eyes suddenly sparkled like Noah Tall's glittery dust. 'That's it!' he said, smiling so broadly his face looked like it might split.

'What's it?' said Pigasus.

Hugo picked up the signpost and stood it up next to the square hole in the ground. He held it upright, his arm straight out at shoulder height.

'There are four different ways we can put this signpost into this hole,' said Hugo. As he spoke he turned the post a quarter-turn. 'But only one is right.'

'I don't mean to be picky, but that's the gist of what we just said,' said Pigasus.

Hugo smiled and spun the signpost another quarter-turn. 'I know,' he said. 'But what you didn't say is that when the signpost is in the ground the right way, it must tell us that back the way we came is the horse-shoe bend in the river.' Hugo turned the post another quarter-turn, so the sign with the Ω symbol on it pointed back down the path they had just come along. 'If that sign is right, then all the others must be right too,' he proclaimed. With a satisfied nod Hugo let the signpost slide into the hole.

'He's right!' said Savage, scampering on top of Hugo's head. 'The boy's a genius.'

Snowdon nodded slowly and smiled. Pigasus still looked puzzled.

'So,' said Hugo, reading the sign, 'we take the path off to the right.'

'That's what I said ten minutes ago!' said Pigasus.

'I think that might have been a lucky guess,' observed Snowdon.

'My dear chap,' said Pigasus, 'I can assure you that luck had nothing to do with it.'

'Besides,' said Hugo, 'one man's lucky guess is another man's keen instinct.'

'Thank you, Hugo,' said Pigasus. 'I often find I can almost *smell* the solution to a problem.'

'I'm not surprised, with those nostrils,' said Savage.

Hugo looked up at the sky. The sun had long since

passed directly overhead and was now sliding ever nearer the horizon. It would soon be dusk. His pulse quickened and he felt his tummy fluttering with panic.

'We have to hurry,' Hugo said. 'There's no time to lose.'

Chapter 33

As they walked over gently rolling hills and across fields of ochre and emerald, Snowdon scanned the scenery for buffalogres. Pigasus surveyed the undergrowth for any signs of food. Savage rode on Hugo's shoulder, and together they studied the sky. They watched as the sun edged five, ten, fifteen degrees through its arc and still there was no sign of the next location on Pedro's map.

Then the path stopped dead. All that lay ahead was open countryside. Hugo scratched his head and sighed. 'What now?'

'Er . . . I'm just going to pick some jamberries,' said Pigasus anxiously. With a few bounds he was among some nearby trees, shaking fruit from their boughs.

'Food is always the answer for Pigasus,' observed Snowdon with a wry smile. 'Now, let's rest for a while. A tired body means a tired mind.'

Hugo took out his notebook and opened it at the map of the island. He drew in the ring of Tanglefoot Forest and the tree stump where they'd met Noah Tall. He sketched the distinctive bend in the river where they'd battled the water slugs and he used a dashed line to denote the path they had been following.

'I lied about why I followed you into the forest,' said Snowdon.

Hugo looked up from his map.

Snowdon continued. 'The real reason is that I was moved by what you said about never giving up. You reminded me of my father. He always taught me how important it is to keep trying, no matter how slim the chance of victory might be.'

'I'm glad you came,' said Hugo.

Snowdon nodded. 'So am I.'

Hugo took the piece of wood with Pedro's map out of his satchel. Savage scampered down his arm and perched on the back of his hand, his whiskery nose twitching at the symbols.

'This is impossible,' said Savage. 'Where's Noah Tall when you need him?'

'He would be here if we needed him,' said Snowdon. 'Maybe the fact that he isn't suggests we are on the right lines.'

'Isn't that just wishful thinking?'

'I prefer to call it positive thinking,' said Snowdon. 'I suppose it depends which way you choose to look at it.'

Snowdon's words made Hugo's mind travel back to the night he'd sat on the deck of *El Tonto Perdido* studying the stars with his uncle. Walter had shown him how the Plough could also be seen as the Great Bear. He'd told Hugo, 'As a mapmaker you must always remember that there's more than one way of looking at things.'

Hugo looked again at Pedro's map. He turned it in his hands, reading the symbols upside down. Then he turned the wood so that he was reading the symbols from top to bottom.

Hugo froze, then leaped to his feet. His heart was racing and he could hardly breathe, he was so excited.

'Snowdon! Savage! We've been looking at the map the wrong way all along,' said Hugo. 'It's not meant to be read from left to right. It goes from top to bottom. See?' Snowdon immediately saw what their troublesome symbol stood for.

'It's a mountain,' he said. 'Pedro must have hidden the Silver Acorn somewhere on the mountain.'

Pigasus had just returned from his fruit-gathering spree, his arms laden with red and blue jamberries. 'Which mountain?'

'The symbol is a mountain,' said Hugo. 'Look!' He held Pedro's map up longways for Pigasus to see.

'Yes, I follow your logic and applaud you for your clever deduction,' said Pigasus, snorting down a handful of berries. 'But, my dear boy, my question remains, to which of the island's three identical mountains does the map refer?'

Hugo looked up at the mountains. They were all formed out of the same rugged black rock as the cliff face at Violet Cove. They were all steep and pointed and capped with snow. Hugo's heart sank. They would barely have time to scale one peak before nightfall. They would certainly not have time to climb another if their first choice was the wrong one.

'It's a real puzzle,' said Savage, his whiskers twitching even more than usual. 'If only they didn't all have a snowy crown.'

Hugo scooped Savage up in his hand and kissed him square on the nose. 'Savage, you're an absolute star,' he said. 'That's it exactly! The snow is nature's crown.'

Savage blinked in bemusement but his ears fanned out with pride.

'Is there any danger that you're going to explain this revelation?' asked Pigasus.

'The mountain on Pedro's map has snow on top,' said Hugo.

Pigasus looked at Snowdon and rolled his eyes. 'Oh dear me, I think the stress of our expedition has finally got to him,' he said. 'Hugo, old chap, either I'm seeing triple or all three of those mountains have got snow on top.'

But Snowdon understood what Hugo was thinking. 'Pedro would have had to specify which of the mountains his map referred to,' he said. 'That's why he drew it with snow on top.'

'Oh dear, I'm getting a headache,' said Pigasus. 'How many times do I have to repeat myself? ALL THREE MOUNTAINS HAVE GOT SNOW ON TOP!'

Snowdon chuckled at his friend's tantrum. He put an arm round Pigasus to calm him down. 'Pigasus, what time of year is it?'

'Early spring,' said Pigasus, frowning.

'Exactly. During the winter, snow falls on all the mountains. By this time of year the snowcaps on the mountains have barely started to melt,' explained Snowdon. 'But when Pedro stole the Silver Acorn it was early summer. At that time of year most of the snow would have melted.'

'But the highest peak is always the first and the last to have snow on top,' said Hugo. 'That's why it's nature's crown.'

Now a smile of understanding was beginning to curl the corners of Pigasus's mouth. His ears pricked up and he nodded slowly.

'So, when Pedro drew the map, only the highest peak had snow on top,' explained Hugo.

'So what you're saying,' said Pigasus, already chuckling to himself, 'is that only one mountain had been *snowed on*, Snowdon.'

'Come on, Pigasus,' said Hugo. '*Snow* time for jokes.'

'I think Pedro hid the Silver Acorn at the top of that mountain,' said Snowdon, pointing to the highest of the three peaks. The sun was low and the air was getting cold. Wisps of cloud were passing across the sky, momentarily hiding the tip of the highest mountain.

'Spooky,' said Pigasus.

'We'd better hurry if we're going to climb it before the half-moon rises,' said Snowdon.

'Right to the very top?' said Pigasus.

'All the way,' said Snowdon.

'Don't the buffalogres live in those mountains?'

'Scores of them.'

'So couldn't we go and rescue Uncle Walter from their cave on the way?' Hugo pleaded.

'It's not that simple,' said Snowdon. 'He'll be guarded by hordes of buffalogres. We can't just waltz in and pick him up. Our priority is to find the Silver Acorn. When that is done peace will return to the island and everyone will be safe.'

'I just thought if we were going to be passing the cave . . .'

'No.'

CHapter 34

The sides of the mountain were too steep to allow the companions to head straight for the top, so they had to pick a zigzag path towards the summit. The hillside was covered in rough black shingle that slipped underfoot. It was a challenge not to fall on the treacherous slope, and every stride required huge effort. To make matters worse, an icy wind whipped against them.

Hugo was cold and tired. He made a slit in the middle of one of the blankets from his satchel and put it over his head like a cape, but still the wind gnawed at his flesh. His face and hands were raw and his lungs were fighting for breath. How he would have loved to swap places with Savage, who was nestled in the warmth of his tunic pocket.

'What are we looking for when we get to the top?' Hugo shouted to Snowdon, but his voice was carried away by the howling wind. He quickened his step just enough to catch up with Snowdon and tug at his fur. Snowdon stopped and looked down at Hugo, turning his head away from the wind.

Snowdon's long fur was almost horizontal, like a flag. As his fringe flapped away from his face Hugo saw his eyes for the first time ever. They were shaped like a cat's – bright orange with black slits for pupils.

Hugo repeated his question.

'According to the map, we must look for something shaped like a black triangle,' instructed Snowdon. 'Maybe a rock or some kind of marking on the ground. We must hurry though.'

The sun was almost at the horizon, streaking the sky with orange and pink light. It would soon be dark.

Suddenly Snowdon ducked behind a boulder. He signalled for Hugo and Pigasus to tuck in behind him. Savage peeped out from under Hugo's cape.

'About thirty paces up ahead is an entrance to the buffalogres' warren,' whispered Snowdon. He paused to peer round the rock. Then he continued, 'It's no good trying to enter the cave. The maze within is too complicated – too vast. It's said you could spend a lifetime walking around the buffalogres' labyrinth and never find your way out. The important thing is for us to continue to the summit.'

'How do you know it's an entrance to the buffalogres' labyrinth?' asked Pigasus. 'Isn't it possible that it's just any old cave?'

Snowdon shook his head. 'I can tell it's a buffalogres' cave for two reasons,' he said. 'Firstly their tunnels are a distinctive shape – an almost perfect semicircle. The cave up ahead is exactly that shape.'

'That could be a coincidence,' said Pigasus.

'The second reason is that there's a buffalogre guarding the entrance.'

'I see.' Pigasus nodded as though carefully considering the evidence. 'For argument's sake let's assume it *is* the buffalogres' labyrinth. How on earth are we going to get past it alive?'

'Well,' said Snowdon, 'either we can go back and find another way up the mountain, or we can try to sneak past the entrance.'

'We do have a third option,' said Savage. 'I could sneak over to the buffalogre and take him out.'

'Take him out?' repeated Pigasus.

'You know, eliminate him,' said Savage. 'Incapacitate, disable, immobilize him.'

Pigasus looked at Savage with an expression of utter confusion.

'I'll knock him out,' explained Savage slowly.

'My dear little friend,' laughed Pigasus, 'I know very well *what* "take him out" means. I was simply baffled as to *how* you plan to knock him out.'

'Easily,' said Savage. 'I'll creep up on to his head. Then . . . KAPOW.'

'Kapow?' echoed Pigasus.

'Kapow,' said Savage, miming a chopping motion with one clenched paw. 'One swift blow to the head and the buffalogre will be out cold. It'll be swift and pain-less – he won't feel a thing.'

'That's precisely what I'm afraid of,' said Pigasus.

'It's a good plan, Savage,' said Hugo. 'I just think it's best if we don't draw attention to ourselves.'

'Exactly,' agreed Pigasus. 'Stealth is the key.'

'And as we don't have time to go back,' said Hugo, 'we'll have to sneak past.'

'I agree,' said Snowdon. 'The buffalogre seems to be asleep – probably saving energy for tonight's feast. We just have to get past without waking Sleeping Beauty. Follow me, and stay close.'

The rotten-egg stench of the buffalogre turned Hugo's stomach as they approached. He kept as close as he could to Snowdon, his feet slipping on the loose shingle.

Hugo told himself not to look at the sleeping mon-ster – but he couldn't help peeking as they crept past. The creature was sitting on a boulder, slumped forward with its chin on its chest. Its two thick arms hung limply at its sides. Its black nostril pumped steam into the air with every odious breath. Its mouth was gaping slightly and a thick purple tongue lolled out of one side like a huge piece of raw liver. A thick column of drool hung from its hairy chin like a glassy stalactite.

Hugo thought the beast looked strangely peaceful. Hideously ugly, of course, but peaceful.

He and Snowdon were almost past the sleeping sentry when he felt something brush the back of his leg. He turned to see Pigasus lying almost flat against the hillside. He had lost his footing and was scrambling frantically to get up. The more he scrabbled at the loose stones, the more they cascaded down the mountainside.

Hugo tried to signal to Pigasus to stay calm, but it was too late. His frantic attempt to find purchase on the shingle was causing a landslide. Rocks and pebbles bounced and tumbled down the steep slope.

Just as Pigasus felt he was about to lose his grip completely he blindly made one last lunge. To his relief his hoof gripped something that didn't slide away under his weight.

Hugo watched in horror as Pigasus grabbed hold of the buffalogre's foot. The monster's head snapped up, its pink milky eyes suddenly alert. In a flash, the beast reached down and grabbed Pigasus's leg with its powerful claws, dragging him back up the slope with little effort. Hugo's stomach twisted as he watched Pigasus hanging from the monster's grip, kicking and punching the air and desperately flapping his little wings. The buffalogre licked its lips with its fat livery tongue.

Hugo turned and shouted to Snowdon to come and help. But Snowdon was heading up the mountain and Hugo's voice was carried away on the wind. It was up to him to do something before Pigasus was added to the menu for the Half-moon Feast.

Hugo charged at the monster, drawing his sword as he covered the ground between them. He thrust his blade at the buffalogre, piercing its flesh just below its left buttock. The monster turned to look at him. It seemed more annoyed than threatened by the attack – like a dog being irritated by a flea.

As if considering whether or not Hugo was edible, the beast cocked its head to one side and its brow creased into a curious frown. Its breath rattled in its throat. Its eyes didn't blink.

With its free paw the buffalogre reached down and squeezed Hugo's shoulder between its thumb and forefinger. Then it poked him in the stomach. Winded, Hugo groaned and doubled over.

Savage leaped from Hugo's shoulder and disappeared into the thick wiry fur on the buffalogre's arm. A moment later he reappeared on top of the buffalogre's head. 'KAPOW!' he cried as he thumped the monster's skull. 'KAPOW! KAPOW!'

The buffalogre didn't flinch.

Hugo stared into its gaping nostril, a twitching, fleshy tunnel of doom. He could tell the monster was smelling him, like one might savour the aroma of a juicy peach just before gobbling it up. The rage and terror mixing inside Hugo suddenly exploded.

'I'M NOT A PEACH!' he screamed, producing his sword from behind his back.

With all his strength Hugo thrust his weapon up the buffalogre's nostril. He stabbed with so much force that the sword, his hand and most of his forearm went up the monster's nose, and into its head.

The buffalogre's pink eyes swivelled wildly in their sockets. Its whole snout wrinkled up and its tongue flopped out. Then its pupils rolled back until its eyes were just pure-white orbs on either side of its massive head. There was a final puff of eggy steam from its nostril, then the buffalogre dropped to its knees and collapsed in a hairy heap on the floor.

Hugo pulled his sword out of the monster's nose. The blade, and most of his arm, was covered in yellow goo streaked and swirled with crimson. Hugo retched at the stench as he wiped the slime off on the buffalogre's coarse fur.

Pigasus, who had been dumped to the ground when the monster had fallen, scrambled to his feet.

'Remind me, Pigasus,' said Savage, 'what was it you were saying about stealth being the key?'

'Exactly,' said Hugo, smiling broadly at his friend. 'I've never seen anything quite so inept as your attempted escape, by the way. An elephant playing a drum would have made less commotion than you did.'

Pigasus smiled wryly. 'Very funny,' he said. 'Tell me, Hugo, what sort of battle cry is, "I'm not a peach"?'

'It was the first thing that came into my head,' said Hugo, feeling his cheeks flush. 'Anyway, are we going to chat all day or shall we try to catch up with Snowdon?'

'Lead on, my saviours,' said Pigasus. 'I'll be right behind you.'

Chapter 35

They met Snowdon coming back down the mountain, having eventually realized that his companions were no longer with him.

'What took you so long?' asked Snowdon.

'I had to hang around while Hugo was having a word with one of the monsters,' said Pigasus.

Taking in Hugo's pale face, Snowdon decided not to ask for further details. 'Come with me,' he said. 'I have something to show you.'

They followed Snowdon a short distance up the mountain, where he led them to the entrance of another cave. This one was much narrower than the last, tapering to a sharp point at the top. Inside, Noah Tall was waiting for them.

'Look who I found,' said Snowdon.

'Welcome,' said Noah. 'Come in and warm your hands.' He gestured to a small campfire that was burning at the back of the cave.

Hugo was relieved to see Noah. He held his palms out to the flames, his fingertips itching as his circulation returned.

'How goes your quest?' said Noah.

'You tell us,' said Snowdon.

Noah smiled serenely.

'Can you at least tell us if the Silver Acorn is at the top of this mountain?' pleaded Hugo.

'Yes, the Silver Acorn is at the very peak of this mountain,' said Noah Tall. 'But consider this, my friends –

'What is cast, but is not a spell?
What weighs nothing, but is not light?
Solve this tricky riddle,
And you'll be free tonight.'

There was a puff of sparkly smoke and he was gone once more.

'This is ridiculous,' said Pigasus. 'We don't have time to mess around with his puzzles – it's nearly dark outside. He just told us the Silver Acorn is at the top of this mountain and I'm going to find it.'

Pigasus marched off. As he reached the mouth of the cave there was an almighty flash of blue light and a loud cracking noise. He was thrown into the air, flying backwards and skidding into a heap at the back of the cave.

'What on earth was that?' said Hugo, comforting Savage, who had leaped on to his trouser leg in shock.

They all peered at the entrance to the cave. There

seemed to be a film of faint yellow light shimmering across the opening.

Snowdon picked up a small rock and tried to toss it out of the cave. Again there was a deafening crack and a flash of blue light. Then the rock was fired back into the cave. It ricocheted off all the walls before it finally came to rest.

'I can't believe it!' said Snowdon, 'Some kind of force field. Noah Tall has fenced us in with his hocus-pocus.'

'Maybe the riddle is the key,' suggested Hugo.

'Or maybe it's just another pointless test,' said Pigasus.

'Well, we don't have a choice,' said Hugo. 'The riddle said if we solve it we will be set free. So let's solve it.'

'What is cast that isn't a spell?' muttered Snowdon to himself.

'Well, you cast iron. And you cast out fishing nets. They aren't spells,' said Savage.

'What about weighing nothing?' said Hugo.

'A net doesn't weigh very much.'

'But it does weigh a little, and it is light. What do you think, Pigasus?'

But Pigasus didn't hear him. He was gazing into the fire, mesmerized by its flames dancing against the darkness of the cave.

'Pigasus?' repeated Hugo.

Pigasus looked up at Hugo. Immediately his hair

stood up all over his body and he gasped. 'Look out, Hugo! Behind you!' he screamed.

Hugo spun round, drawing his sword ready for battle. A huge black figure was lurking behind him. It loomed over him like a giant phantom. It was carrying a sword and looked ready to attack.

Hugo returned his sword to its scabbard and turned back to see Pigasus cowering behind Snowdon, who was chuckling gently to himself.

'That's just my shadow,' said Hugo. 'The shadow cast on the wall is so big because I'm standing close to the fire. Watch this.'

Hugo walked away from the fire and his shadow shrank down until it was no bigger than he was. When he walked back towards the flames, his shadow ballooned.

'I've got it!' exclaimed Hugo. 'What weighs nothing, but isn't light? Well, darkness isn't light, is it? It is the absence of light. And it weighs absolutely nothing.'

'But you don't cast darkness,' said Snowdon.

'True,' agreed Hugo. 'But we all cast something that is a form of darkness.'

'A shadow!' yelped Pigasus. 'We cast a shadow, and a shadow is not light and a shadow weighs nothing!'

As he spoke there was a crackling noise at the mouth of the cave, followed by another blue flash and then the shimmering yellow light was gone.

Snowdon picked up another stone and threw it towards the mouth of the cave. The stone flew into the open and fell silently out of sight.

'Pigasus, you're a genius,' said Hugo generously.

'I'm not just a pretty face, you know,' Pigasus replied with a grin.

'You most certainly are not,' said Savage.

Snowdon was annoyed. 'Solving Noah's riddle has wasted precious time,' he muttered. 'Maybe we were wrong to trust him after all.'

They all ran to the mouth of the cave. A dull whining noise was coming from the ground beneath their feet. It was as if the mountain itself was despairing of their plight.

The sky was dark and the night was lit only by a brilliant white semicircle. The half-moon was rising steadily in an arc over the mountain. Hugo looked out across Tanglefoot Forest in the direction of Violet Cove. He could make out the edge of the clifftop and smoky fog bank – beyond which, he hoped, *El Tonto Perdido* was waiting to take him and Uncle Walter home.

Chapter 36

Admiral Rupert Lilywhite stood on the rear deck of *El Tonto Perdido* admiring the brilliant half-moon. There was only a faint whining noise to disturb the perfect peace of the evening.

'Beautiful evening, ain't it, Admiral?' growled a voice in his ear.

Rupert screamed like a schoolgirl and spun round. Muddle and most of the crew were standing behind him in a sinister huddle.

'Gracious me, Seaman Muddle,' said Rupert. 'What is the meaning of this?'

'Me and the men were just wondering if you fancied taking a stroll?' Oliver Muddle grinned.

'A stroll? Where on earth to?'

Oliver Muddle drew his sword and pointed it at Rupert. 'All the way to the end of a plank.'

Admiral Lilywhite's mouth fell open. His lip quivered. 'Is this some sort of mutiny, Seaman Muddle?'

'No, sir,' said Muddle. 'Me and the crew have just decided you should be relieved of your command.'

'But that's exactly what a mutiny is,' said Rupert uncertainly.

There was a murmur of surprise among the sailors. 'Oh,' said Oliver Muddle. 'In that case, aye, sir, consider this a mutiny.'

Rockford grabbed Rupert and held his arms behind his back. Rusty and Swipe tied him up and Muddle prodded him with his sword to guide him towards the plank they had lashed to the balustrade around the main deck. It protruded about four feet over the ocean.

Rupert stepped on to the rough piece of timber. Muddle poked him with his sword again and he walked gingerly along the board. The plank groaned and flexed under Rupert's weight. The sea below sloshed against the boat like lashings of black ink. Rupert began to cry, his tears leaving two pink trails in his white face powder.

'Why are you doing this?' he said, turning to face his crew. 'I thought we were all getting along splendidly.'

'But we know for a fact that you plan to take all the credit for this expedition. And we've had enough of waiting for the mapmaker – *we want to go home.*'

'Yeah, I'm bored,' grumbled Bandit. 'If I'd known we were going to be away this long, I'd have brought a good book.'

'And this constant sunshine is playing havoc with my skin,' complained Hawkeye. 'I've aged years on this ship.'

'I miss my mummy,' sniffed Rockford, his huge

biceps bulging as he dabbed his eyes with a tiny hanky. 'What if we fall off the end of the world and I never see her again?'

'Fine,' said Rupert. 'We'll sail for home right this minute. Now, who wants to navigate?'

The sailors looked at each other.

'You see,' said Rupert, 'we need the mapmaker to get home. We have to wait for him.' Sensing a reprieve, Rupert took a step towards the ship.

Immediately Oliver Muddle raised his sword. 'Not so fast,' he said. 'I spoke to the crew this afternoon and they all want me to take over command of this voyage. I may well decide to wait for the mapmaker – but that's a decision I'll make once you are off my ship.'

'So you've gone over my head to whip the rug from under me?' said Admiral Lilywhite. 'If you were going to stab me in the back, you could at least have done it to my face.'

Oliver Muddle frowned.

'The thing is,' said Rusty Cleaver, wagging a huge knife at Rupert as he spoke, 'you think you're better than us just because you got loads of money.'

'That's absolutely not true,' insisted Rupert. 'I think I'm better than you because I have beautiful clothes and a decent education and impeccable personal hygiene . . .' He trailed off as he noticed the expressions on the sailors' faces.

'We're men of principle,' said Muddle, pressing the tip of his blade against Rupert's chest. 'We can't take orders from someone we don't respect, and you don't get our respect just because your daddy has lots of money. You can't buy respect, you see.'

'I'll double everyone's wages if you don't kill me,' said Rupert.

Oliver Muddle turned to Rockford and gave him a single nod. Rockford reached out, grabbed Rupert by the scruff of his neck . . . and pulled him back on deck.

Oliver Muddle grinned. 'Welcome aboard, Admiral,' he said.

Then a monstrous scream tore through the night.

CHapter 37

The high-pitched moan beneath Hugo's feet erupted into a chilling scream. He understood immediately what was happening. The buffalogres within the labyrinth of tunnels were preparing for their Half-moon Feast, and they were singing for their supper.

'We have to hurry,' urged Hugo.

He looked up at the summit of the mountain. They were just approaching the snowline. Their progress from here onwards would be even slower and more treacherous than it had been already. It would take them hours to reach the top. How had Pedro managed all those years ago?

'Wait!' Hugo yelled. 'Wait a minute. Why did Pedro climb this mountain?'

'What do you mean?' said Snowdon.

'Pedro was trying to escape from Erebus,' said Hugo, his thoughts becoming clearer. 'He wanted to get off the island with the Silver Acorn. So why would he have climbed all the way to the top of this mountain to hide it here? Wouldn't he have made straight for the Violet Cove?'

'No one knows what Pedro was thinking,' said

Snowdon. 'Why did he hide the acorn at all? Why not take it with him? Everything about Pedro is a mystery.'

'Noah Tall told us himself that the Silver Acorn was at the peak of this mountain,' said Pigasus.

'Exactly!' said Hugo. The pieces of the puzzle were falling into place. 'Noah told us the acorn was at the peak of the mountain, but he never gives a straight answer. That's rule number one. He told us that the first time we met him.'

'Why should we pay any attention to what Noah says after he trapped us in that cave with his pointless shadow riddle?' growled Snowdon.

'It wasn't pointless though,' said Hugo. 'It was another part of the clue. Look down there.' Hugo pointed down the hillside at the valley below, bathed in pale blue moonshine. 'How would you describe the shadow of this mountain?'

'It's a big black triangle,' said Pigasus.

'And what shape is the next symbol on Pedro's map?'

'A black triangle,' said Savage, leaping excitedly on to Hugo's shoulder.

'Look at the next two symbols together,' said Hugo. 'They represent this mountain – and its shadow!'

'The Silver Acorn *is* at the peak of this mountain,' he said, grinning. 'But at the peak of its shadow, not the summit itself.'

Snowdon looked at the shadows of the mountains and thought about Hugo's idea. The peak of the highest mountain's shadow fell close to the horseshoe bend in the river. If Pedro had crossed the river there and headed straight for Violet Cove, he would have met the tip of the shadow before re-entering the forest.

'When the moon is directly over this mountain, its shadow will point to the Silver Acorn,' said Hugo.

'You're right!' said Snowdon. 'It makes perfect sense.' He gave Hugo a pat on the back so powerful Hugo nearly collapsed.

'Well, what are we waiting for?' said Pigasus, and he bounded off down the steep hillside.

Snowdon and Hugo followed – leaping downhill with big, energetic strides. Savage clung to Hugo's cape with his two front paws while his body and tail flew out behind like a furry streamer. The loose stones gave way under every footstep, sending rocks and pebbles bouncing down the mountainside. It was much quicker bounding and sliding down the mountain than it had been trudging up – and much more fun.

Whooping and laughing, they were like children at the beach slipping and jumping down a giant sand dune. The end of their quest was in sight and their troubles would soon be behind them. They had forgotten all about vampire beetles and three-headed snakes and flesh-eating water slugs. They had even forgotten all about the dangers of the three-horned, razor-toothed, eggy-breathed monsters preparing for their feast inside the mountain.

Then they ran smack into a pack of buffalogres making their way up the hill towards them.

CHAPTER 38

Pigasus ran into them first. He was too busy watching his trotters on the loose stones to look where he was going. He brushed past one, then ran square into another. It was like slamming into a hairy brick wall, and he dropped into a dazed heap on the ground. Snowdon was too close behind to stop himself, and followed his friend into the midst of the monsters. Hugo skidded on the loose rocks, slid right through one buffalogre's legs and bumped into Snowdon. Savage was catapulted through the air, landing on his tummy with a small thud.

The buffalogres formed a wide ring round them. Some dropped on to all fours and stalked like hunting cats, others stayed upright. Snowdon, Pigasus and Hugo stood warily with their backs together, eyeing the monsters surrounding them. Savage scampered over and sheltered between Hugo's legs.

The beasts snorted and drooled, their eyes wild with delight. A few of them threw their heads back and let out a skin-pimpling screech – it was like the sound of fingernails on slate but a hundred times as loud. Others joined in and soon all of them were making the horrific sound.

'Now, I'm no expert on buffalogres,' shouted Pigasus, struggling to make himself heard, 'but something tells me they're not offering us a friendly invitation to join their feast.'

'What do we do now?' croaked Hugo. His mouth was so dry he could hardly speak.

'I think it might be a good time to draw your weapons,' said Snowdon. He reached over his shoulder and gripped the hilt of his broadsword. Hugo drew his sword and Snowdon produced his cactus spine. Pigasus didn't move.

'You too, Pigasus,' urged Snowdon. 'Draw your bow and be ready to shoot like you've never shot before.'

Slowly Pigasus slipped his bow off his shoulder. 'I have a confession to make,' he said as his trembling hoofs fed an arrow into the bow. 'I'm honestly not really a very good shot at all. I wasn't really aiming for the three-headed snake in the forest – I was aiming for the vampire beetle that was attacking Hugo. And I was actually trying to hit those water slugs by the river – I had no idea Hugo wanted me to miss them.'

'I have a confession to make too,' said Snowdon. 'We knew that all along.' The buffalogres were closing in on them. 'But in a second or two those ugly beasts are going to be so close a blind man on a galloping donkey wouldn't be able to miss.'

Snowdon, Hugo, Savage and Pigasus held their weapons at the ready. The buffalogres prowled around them. The air stank of rotten eggs.

One of the monsters leaped. It moved as fast as a lion. Hugo saw it coming and took a step backwards, but Snowdon lunged forward, swinging his sword in two hands above his head. The buffalogre was still in mid-air when Snowdon's blade sliced through it, splitting its head open right down the middle. The monster dropped heavily to the ground, oozing slime and blood over the pebbles.

The other buffalogres screeched louder than ever. Hugo felt his whole body shaking. There seemed to be no escape, but this was his chance to make his father proud. 'Never give up,' Hugo told himself, clasping his pendant. 'Never give up.'

Two more beasts leaped at the friends, teeth and tongues and wild eyes shining in the moonlight. Snowdon spun round, wielding his sword at waist height, and sliced one buffalogre right across its belly. Whining like a dog, the monster skulked back into the pack. At the same time, the second buffalogre landed on Snowdon's back. He dropped to a crouched position and for a moment Hugo thought his friend had fallen. Then, with a resonant roar, Snowdon stood up forcefully, throwing off his attacker. The buffalogre flew backwards, its legs flailing, and landed in a heap. Before the monster had a chance to get to its feet, Snowdon turned and ran his sword through its heart.

Pigasus drew back his bow, aimed at one of the seemingly endless tide of predators and let an arrow fly. It shot off at an angle and missed the monster by at least ten feet, but luckily it hit another buffalogre right between the eyes, killing it just as it was about to pounce on Hugo.

Hugo was unaware of his lucky escape because he was otherwise occupied – with yet another beast. As before, he hid his sword behind his back and waited for the monster to get up close. Its twitching round nostril was like a big target in the middle of its face.

'When will you lot get the message – I AM NOT A PEACH?' With that, Hugo gripped his sword tightly and rammed it right up the buffalogre's nose and into its head. The monster whinnied pathetically, dropped to its knees and fell flat on its face. Hugo just managed to jump out of the way before the dying beast squashed him completely.

'Bullseye!' shouted Hugo.

'I think you mean buffalogre's nose,' laughed Savage. But his smile faded as he saw yet another buffalogre snatch Hugo from behind. The monster lifted him up by the scruff of his neck and turned to leave. Hugo's legs kicked at empty air and his sword swung at nothing.

Savage scampered past the retreating buffalogre and positioned himself in its path. Striking a defiant pose with his cactus spike aloft, he shouted at the approaching monster, 'Put him down, or I'll put *you* down.'

His heart was in his mouth as he waited for his mighty duel.

But the buffalogre neither heard nor saw Savage. It stepped over him and continued up the mountain.

Determined to save his friend, Savage scampered after the buffalogre again. This time he opted for a different tactic and leaped on to its ankle as it walked. Turning so that he was looking at the ground, he gripped the beast's coarse fur with three paws. With his fourth he rammed his trusty cactus spine deep into the monster's heel.

The buffalogre belched out a gruesome screech and hopped to a stop, dropping Hugo in the process. While it nursed its agonizing splinter, Hugo quickly scooped Savage into his pocket and ran back to Pigasus.

The three of them scanned the hillside from left to right and back again.

'I think they've gone,' gasped Hugo.

'We must have scared them off,' said Pigasus confidently.

They turned to share the good news with Snowdon. That was when they realized how wrong they were.

While Pigasus, Hugo and Savage had been fighting off a few buffalogres each, the rest of the pack had been concentrating their attentions on Snowdon. The monsters had formed a tight ring round him and were circling slowly. Every now and then two or three would pounce at once. Claws flashed, battle cries split the air and Snowdon's sword repeatedly cut through the monsters. Dead buffalogres were strewn across the ground – their tongues lolling on to the pebbles and their eyes white.

Snowdon was standing – but only just. His head hung low and his shoulders were limp. He was holding his sword with one hand, struggling to lift its heavy blade. His other arm was clutching his stomach, where blood flowed from a wound, staining his silver fur and forming a dark red pool at his feet.

Hugo pushed into the crowd of monsters, slashing his sword at their legs and feet to no avail.

'Snowdon!' he yelled, flooded by despair. 'Snowdon!'

'Go with Pigasus,' Snowdon replied. He was short of breath and his words came slowly. 'Find the Silver Acorn. I will fight on here, but you must finish our quest.'

'I'm not leaving you,' called Hugo angrily.

'We have to go,' Savage urged, scampering up to Hugo's shoulder. 'Our only hope is to find the Silver Acorn.'

Hugo hated to leave Snowdon at the mercy of the monsters, but he knew Savage was right. Hot tears filled his eyes as he battled his way out of the vicious horde and ran back to Pigasus.

'We have to get the acorn,' said Hugo. He began to make his way down the mountain.

'Wait!' said Pigasus. 'Climb on my back. And hold on tight.'

Pigasus got down on all fours and Hugo climbed on and sat astride his shoulders, behind his bow and quiver of arrows. Savage took his place astride Hugo's shoulders, clutching his blond curls.

'Ready,' said Hugo, taking hold of two fistfuls of fur.

Pigasus took a deep breath and began to flap his wings. Hugo and Savage held on tight. Nothing happened.

Pigasus stopped flapping and took a few deep breaths.

'In your own time,' said Savage, eyeing a single buffalogre that had started making its way over to them.

'Come on!' cried Hugo. 'The whole island needs us to make it!'

Pigasus flapped and flapped.

Hugo's heart thumped.

He felt Pigasus lifting off the ground, just a fraction. Now galloping at full speed the buffalogre lunged for them, baring its fangs and claws. Just as the beast's grasp closed around Pigasus, he lifted off the ground and soared into the night sky. A deep frown creased the buffalogre's brow as it tried to understand where its prey had disappeared to.

'You did it!' shouted Hugo. 'We're flying!'

But when Hugo looked back at the hillside below his elation turned sour. Snowdon was watching them fly away. For a moment he held his sword aloft, daring another buffalogre to try to attack him. Then he did something that Hugo didn't expect. Snowdon lay his sword down on the ground. The buffalogres hesitated, as if they thought this was some kind of trap. Snowdon raised an arm in a gesture of surrender and dropped to his knees.

The buffalogres pounced as one. Within seconds Snowdon had been knocked unconscious and was being dragged up the hillside by his ankles. Soon he would be taken through the entrance to the cave and deep inside the labyrinth.

Hugo turned away. He couldn't watch his friend being dragged off like a sack of coal. Until now Snowdon had been incredibly brave and noble, and he couldn't understand why he had just given up.

On the slope below, one lone buffalogre was watching Pigasus fly away, still intrigued by the flapping pig that had slipped through its claws. Glancing back at the rest of the pack, it half turned as if going to join its clan. Then it stopped, turned back and, with a defiant snort, set off down the mountain.

Chapter 39

Hugo saw something pass across the sky above them. At first he thought he had imagined it. Then he heard the slow, heavy flap of broad wings.

'I think we've got company,' Hugo said. 'It's a scavagor.'

'Brilliant news,' said Pigasus. He was flapping so hard his little wings were a blur, and he was panting heavily with the strain.

With his left hand Hugo took an extra-firm grip of Pigasus's scruff. He scanned the sky overhead, searching for the rat-bird that was circling them. It was a clear night and millions of stars speckled the sky.

'You're mine, you're mine,' the scavagor squawked as it swooped.

Gripping Pigasus with his knees, Hugo paused, then released his fistful of fur and drew his sword, grasping it in both hands. With all his strength he thrust his sword upwards until his arms were extended straight above his head. There was a hideous squawk followed by frantic flapping. Hugo watched the scavagor fall silently to the ground – tumbling clumsily as it disappeared from sight.

'That was a clever ploy – drawing your sword at the last second,' said Savage, clutching on to Hugo's hair.

'Well, that scavagor certainly seemed to fall for it,' said Hugo.

Glancing back, he saw the half-moon sitting directly over the mountain. Up ahead he noticed a tree growing right at the point of the triangular shadow. 'We're nearing the tip of the shadow,' Hugo said. 'I bet Pedro buried the acorn under that tree.'

Pigasus had started to descend. As they neared the ground he began to cycle his legs in mid-air, just as he had done the day they'd met.

Hugo could feel Savage's claws pulling his hair more tightly as they braced themselves for the landing. The ground met them with a thud. Pigasus took a couple of steps but they were travelling too fast for his legs to keep up. He tripped and fell on to his tummy, skidding at speed across the rough grass and ploughing a furrow with his snout. Eventually they came to a halt directly under the tree, Pigasus's nose just inches from its thick trunk.

'Well, well,' said Pigasus, shaking some loose earth from his ears. 'That's two good landings out of two for us, Hugo. You must be my lucky charm.'

Hugo would have disagreed with his friend's assessment of his flying skills, but he was mesmerized by something else. He was staring at the mound of dirt that Pigasus had churned up as they'd landed. At the top of the wedge of freshly tilled earth, right next to the tree, something was glinting.

Hugo leaped off Pigasus's back and rushed over to see what they'd uncovered, but when he picked up the object his hope turned to confusion. He wasn't holding the Silver Acorn. He was holding a diamond that almost covered the palm of his hand.

Tossing the precious stone to one side, Hugo dropped to his knees and began digging in the soil. As he scraped the earth away his eyes widened.

'Look at this!' he gasped.

Pigasus peered over his shoulder and his eyes opened even wider.

Chapter 40

The ground was full of treasure.

Pigasus used his sharp trotters like trowels and they quickly uncovered the shallow hole containing Pedro's riches. Savage and Pigasus leaned against the tree trunk and surveyed what they had found. A thick gold chain was coiled up next to Hugo like a golden mountain.

'Something tells me Pedro's deepest desire was to be rich,' said Hugo.

'Looks like his dream came true,' said Savage, sitting atop a Roman soldier's helmet made of solid gold.

'But it didn't last for long,' said Hugo, scooping up a handful of precious stones. 'He'd never have escaped carrying all this treasure.'

'It just goes to show though – the Silver Acorn never fails,' said Pigasus, admiring his reflection in a golden breastplate. 'And it works its magic quickly.'

'We have to find it,' said Hugo. 'It must be around here somewhere.'

'We've already dug up the area all round the tree,' said Pigasus. 'There's nowhere else to look.'

'Then we have to dig deeper,' shouted Hugo, clawing

frantically at the earth. 'We can't give up. Not when we're this close.'

'We've dug all we can,' said Pigasus softly, placing a trotter on Hugo's shoulder. 'I've just realized something. Pedro's map doesn't lead to the Silver Acorn. Pedro's map leads to Pedro's treasure.'

'So where's the Silver Acorn then?' asked Hugo defiantly.

Savage jumped on to Hugo's shoulder. 'Maybe Pedro didn't leave it on the island after all,' he said. 'Maybe he kept it all along.'

Hugo tried to absorb the reality of what his friends were saying. Something snorted nearby. Hugo's nose was filled with the ugly stench of rotten eggs. He knew what he would see even before he looked up.

Just a hundred yards away was a buffalogre, galloping towards them with death in its eyes.

Chapter 41

Hugo and Pigasus stood up and backed towards the tree.

'What now?' whispered Pigasus.

'What does it matter?' sighed Hugo angrily. 'Uncle Walter and Snowdon will have been eaten by now. Our only weapon is your bow and arrow, which is erratic to say the very least. No offence.'

'None taken,' said Pigasus. 'But we're not beaten yet. The buffalogres may be savage and merciless hunters, but they are social eaters. They won't start a meal until everyone is ready.'

'You mean that they won't start the Half-moon Feast until our friend returns from hunting us?'

'Exactly,' said Pigasus. 'All we have to do is keep this chap busy, and Snowdon and your uncle will be kept alive. Admittedly they'll still be imprisoned inside an impossibly complicated maze of tunnels – but they will be alive.'

The buffalogre approached, puffing clouds of steam into the sky.

'Once again, it seems that the only way is up. Climb on my back.'

Hugo grabbed hold of his friend's shoulders. Pigasus beat his tired wings as fast as he could. Slowly his trotters left the ground and he took off.

'We'll never get away,' said Hugo. 'You must be exhausted.'

'We're not flying away,' said Pigasus. 'We're just flying up.'

Pigasus lifted Hugo and Savage high into the leafy refuge of the tree. When they reached a sturdy branch Pigasus clambered on to it, gasping for breath. Down on the ground the buffalogre looked up in utter bewilderment.

'What are you waiting for?' mocked Savage. 'Don't tell me you can't climb trees.'

The buffalogre stepped up to the tree trunk. It pressed its palms against the bark and looked up. Its milky eyes fixed on Hugo and Pigasus. Then it started to climb. It kept its belly close to the trunk. It was slithering like a lizard, with its tail snaking behind it.

'Oh. Apparently it can climb trees,' said Savage. 'Rather quickly too.'

Chapter 42

'You have to go higher,' urged Pigasus.

He pushed Hugo up to the next branch.

Hugo climbed from branch to branch as fast as he could. As he got higher the branches became narrower. They were starting to bow under his weight.

'I think my burly frame is just too heavy for these flimsy branches,' said Savage.

Hugo heard Pigasus yelp below him. It was a sound full of despair and it turned Hugo's blood cold. He looked down between his feet. The buffalogre had caught up with Pigasus and was hauling him out of the tree. Pigasus's eyes were wild with terror.

'Go as high as you can,' Pigasus yelled.

Hugo's mind was racing. Hundreds of thoughts crowded into his head. He thought about everybody he would never see again. He thought about Uncle Walter, Pigasus, Snowdon and Delphina. He wondered about Pedro's map.

'I can't believe Pedro's map was just a map to his gold,' he muttered. 'If that's the case, then why would he include an acorn symbol on it?'

Savage yelped. The buffalogre had reached the

ground, where it had pinned Pigasus to the floor with its immense tail. Now, barging its powerful shoulder against the trunk, it was shaking the whole tree.

Hugo was reminded of Pigasus shaking jamberries from a tree on his first night in Shelter Point. He'd buried the pips because he didn't want to insult Pigasus by not eating them. The next morning when he'd collected his satchel the pips had already grown into tall shoots. What if all plant life on the island grew as quickly?

Hugo's branch swayed so far over to one side that he lost his footing. He dangled from the tree by his hands for a second. Desperately he swung his legs up and crossed them round the branch. He clung on with everything he had and tried to finish his train of thought.

What if Pedro *had* buried the Silver Acorn with his gold? Would it have grown quickly in the fertile soil? Snowdon said they'd had heavy rain on the island in recent years. That would have helped to nurture the Silver Acorn. If the acorn had grown, it would have turned into a tree. Hugo looked at the leaves all around him.

'Savage,' he said, 'what sort of tree are we in?'

'This is no time for a horticultural quiz,' said Savage.

'Just answer me.'

Savage glanced quickly at the distinctive wobbly outline of the leaves. 'That's easy,' he said. 'It's an oak tree.'

Delphina had told Hugo the Silver Acorn was picked from the Tree of Hope – a mighty oak tree with a single silver acorn on its branches.

Hugo felt hope coursing through his veins. Was it possible the Silver Acorn had grown into a new Tree of Hope? If so, then it must have produced its own Silver Acorn!

Hugo remembered Noah Tall's words.

When I'm not there to guide or teach
The Silver Acorn will be in your reach

And he saw a glint . . .

. . . nestled at the tip of a twiggy branch above his head, partly hidden by leaves. Hugo stretched one arm up.

His fingers closed round the Silver Acorn.

Chapter 43

'The tree has stopped shaking,' observed Savage.

'Are you two going to stay there all night?' It was Pigasus. 'Because I could really do with a plate of mashed patata and some rotten peaches.'

'Pigasus?' called Hugo. 'Is it safe?'

'Safe? It's absolute heaven,' said Pigasus. 'You are a hero.'

Hugo looked down. The buffalogre was grazing nearby. Its horns were smooth and its eyes chocolate brown; it paid the boy no attention as he climbed down the tree.

When Hugo reached the ground, his hands shaking with joy, Pigasus stood on his hind legs and hugged Hugo to his hairy tummy.

'We're free!' whooped Pigasus. 'You saved us all! I can't believe it, we're finally free. I'm so happy I could kiss you.' Pigasus licked Hugo's cheek with his slobbery tongue.

'Put me down!' laughed Hugo.

'Let me see the Silver Acorn,' said Pigasus.

Hugo held it out and Pigasus whistled.

'Do you want to hold it?' Hugo asked.

'I'd better not,' said Pigasus. 'If my dreams came true, we'd be lost under a mountain of rotten jamberries!'

'You saved us all,' said Savage, nuzzling Hugo's cheek.

But Hugo's mind was elsewhere. 'What about Uncle Walter?' he said. 'We have to go into the buffalogres' labyrinth to find him.'

'I think Snowdon will take care of that,' said Pigasus.

'But Snowdon gave up,' said Hugo. 'I saw him drop his sword and surrender.'

'Are you sure he gave up?' asked Pigasus. 'Or was he just pretending to give up?'

Hugo shrugged. 'Why would Snowdon pretend to give up?'

'Wait and see,' said Pigasus with a wink.

Chapter 44

'Look over there,' said Pigasus. They were about halfway to the river where they'd left Delphina behind. Hugo followed the direction of his finger up the mountainside, and saw a bulky figure coming towards them. As it got closer he realized it was Snowdon. He was walking slowly and carrying something on his back.

'Uncle Walter!' yelled Hugo. He ran towards them.

Snowdon knelt down and Walter slid off his back, ready to greet his nephew. Hugo ran straight into his arms, nearly knocking him over.

'Am I glad to see you!' laughed Walter. 'How's my favourite nephew?'

Hugo couldn't speak for a moment. His uncle was gaunt and pale, but he was overcome with happiness to see him alive.

'I thought I was never going to see you again,' he sobbed. 'First there was that horrible scavagor, then Tanglefoot Forest, then the vampire beetles and the flesh-eating water slugs and the riddles and . . .'

'I know,' said Walter softly. He held Hugo tight. 'You saved my life. Snowdon here has told me all about it.

And I hear you even managed to map the whole island while you were at it!'

'How did you get out of the labyrinth?' asked Hugo. 'I thought you'd be lost in there forever.'

'Between you and me, I thought so too,' replied Walter matter-of-factly. 'When the buffalogres took me deep into the mountain I had no idea what was in store, but I knew I'd never find my own way out. Of course, as soon as I saw the fire I realized they were preparing to eat me – I just didn't know when.

'It felt like I'd been in that cave for an eternity when they brought Snowdon in, and suddenly it seemed to be time for the feast to start. He whispered to me not to worry, but then one of those beasts started dragging me towards the fire, and I have to confess that I was starting to panic. As I got closer and closer to the bonfire the intense heat seemed to be blistering my cheeks and scorching my arms. When I felt the flames singeing my moustache I was sure I was about to be roasted.

'Then, without warning, the buffalogres became placid. They lost interest in cooking me altogether and began ambling around on all fours, nibbling at tufts of grass. Snowdon realized immediately that you had found the Silver Acorn, Hugo, and he carried me to safety.'

Hugo nodded and smiled at his uncle. Then he looked at Snowdon. 'How did you find your way back out of the labyrinth?' he said grudgingly. 'It looked to me like you'd given up the fight.'

'I followed the trail I'd left on the way in,' said Snowdon.

'How did you leave a trail without the buffalogres noticing?'

'I was bleeding heavily,' said Snowdon. 'I knew that if the buffalogres took me to their den I would leave a trail of blood. That's why I pretended to surrender.'

Hugo felt ashamed. 'I thought you had given up,' he said. 'I was really angry with you. I'm sorry.'

Snowdon smiled. 'We all misunderstand others sometimes.'

There was a squeal of delight from further up the hillside. They turned to see a baby mammoth galloping down the mountainside. It was grinning and waving its trunk with excitement. Snowdon smiled and waved back.

'You're still bleeding badly, Snowdon,' said Walter.

'We'd better hurry back to Shelter Point,' said Pigasus.

'There's no need to worry about me. I'll live,' said Snowdon.

'Who says I was worrying about you?' said Pigasus. 'I want to get back for breakfast. I'm starving!'

Delphina was waiting for them at the boat. She had used up both rotten eggs to repel the water slugs. They had been returning to attack her again when Hugo had found the Silver Acorn.

'They suddenly turned round and wriggled away,' she said. 'I guessed straight away that you must have succeeded – I always knew you would.'

They climbed into the boat and Snowdon rowed them across the river. Even Tanglefoot Forest had lost its threatening atmosphere. The trees seemed to be less densely packed, and blue moonlight filtered through the leaves. Vivid flowers were already budding under the canopy. Hugo passed within yards of two vampire beetles, but they took no notice of him. They were too busy feasting – on a gorse bush. Overhead he noticed a scavagor soaring in lazy circles high above the treetops. 'You're free, you're free,' it squawked.

The next morning the gang celebrated with a feast of fried eel and mashed patatas. Dessert was peaches and jamberries. They all ate until their bellies couldn't hold any more food.

Hugo looked around at his companions and he felt warm inside. He couldn't imagine a more unusual collection of characters, and he couldn't imagine having better friends.

'So have you decided what you're going to do with the Silver Acorn?' asked Kramer, wiping his mouths.

'You are entitled to reign over the island as Prince Hugo,' said Pigasus.

Hugo looked at Walter.

'It's your choice, Hugo,' said Walter.

At last Hugo spoke. 'I'm honoured by the offer,' he said, 'but even though I'll miss you all terribly, I can't stay. The world is full of exciting places to explore and lands I want to map. There are so many more paths to travel and I'm just starting to get a taste for adventure.'

'Heaven help us all!' laughed Walter, his eyes crinkling.

'We understand,' said Delphina sadly. 'We'll miss you too.'

'Obviously I can't take the Silver Acorn with me,' said Hugo, 'so I would like to pass it on to Snowdon to help him rule this island. He is noble and brave, just like his father, Prince Erebus.'

Snowdon was taken aback. 'How did you know?'

'You have inherited his strength and you have his fire in your eyes,' said Hugo. 'Besides which, his name is on the dagger you lent me.'

Snowdon threw his head back and roared with laughter.

'Is this true, Snowdon?' asked Delphina. 'Why didn't you tell us?'

'I suppose I didn't think I was worthy of being a

prince,' said Snowdon softly. 'And I didn't want any special treatment just because Erebus was my father.'

'Your father would be proud.' Delphina smiled.

'I agree,' said Pigasus, snorting away tears. 'You have proved yourself to be a worthy successor to his throne.'

Delphina slipped the Silver Acorn on to a leather string and tied it round Snowdon's neck.

'I pronounce you Prince Snowdon,' she said, and everyone cheered.

As the others celebrated, Pigasus made his way over to Hugo.

'My dear boy, life won't be the same around here without you,' he whispered.

'I'll miss you too,' said Hugo.

'Who said anything about missing you?' laughed Pigasus, nudging Hugo playfully with his snout. 'I'm looking forward to a bit of peace and quiet.'

'Maybe we'll bump into each other again one day,' said Hugo, scratching his friend's ear.

'And flutterhogs might fly,' laughed Pigasus. 'Take care, Hugo. And thank you.'

Snowdon turned to Hugo and Walter. 'We'll be sorry to see you leave,' he said. 'But I would ask that you keep our island secret from the outside world.'

'Don't worry about that,' said Walter. 'I know exactly how we can guarantee your privacy.'

Chapter 45

They could see the shape of *El Tonto Perdido* looming through the mist. Walter began rowing the boat as fast as he could.

'Help, help!' screamed Hugo.

The sailors on the ship were drinking and sun-bathing when they heard Hugo's cries. One or two of them staggered to the stern to see what was happening. Rupert rushed from his cabin, extending his telescope at the ready.

When the sailors looked over the side of the ship they were dumbstruck. They saw Hugo and Walter in the rowing boat, being chased by the most hideous beast. It was long and slimy with a knobbly back and ferocious teeth. As it swam closer they realized it was a two-headed crocodile.

'Sea monsters!' screamed Rupert, cowering behind Rockford.

'Throw the ladder down,' shouted Walter. 'There's more of them coming.'

'Not until you show me what you've found,' Rupert called back, his voice shrill with terror. 'Otherwise why should I risk those crocs coming aboard and munching us all?'

'We've got the map,' replied Hugo. 'With this proof of your discovery you are sure to be rich and famous.'

'What are you waiting for, Seaman Whateveryour-nameis?' snapped Rupert. 'Throw them the blasted ladder.'

Hawkeye lowered a rope ladder over the side of the boat. Hugo and Walter climbed up and jumped on to the ship's deck, trying to look terrified by their ordeal. The sailors gathered round to hear their tale.

Firstly, Walter handed a piece of parchment to Rupert.

'Here's your map, Admiral,' he said.

It was a fictitious map they had sketched that morning. It made no mention of the Silver Acorn, or the Tree of Hope, or indeed Tanglefoot Forest. Walter had marked some coordinates in the bottom right-hand corner of the map. If anyone had tried to return to the island using the coordinates, they would have found themselves five hundred miles away from Prince Snowdon's kingdom.

Hugo had completed his own map of the island, annotating the semicircular entrance to the buffal-ogres' labyrinth with a sketch of one of the three-horned monsters. Similarly he had labelled the narrow cave where Noah Tall had given his last clue, complete with a cartoon drawing of their guide. The map now showed the three conical mountains casting three triangular shadows across the island towards the river. He had sketched the Tree of Hope, growing at the tip of the longest shadow, which fell close to a horseshoe-shaped bend in the stream. At the tree's roots Hugo had detailed some gold coins and on one of its branches he'd drawn the Silver Acorn. Then he had tucked the map into his notebook, at the very bottom of his satchel.

'This map's a bit sketchy,' said Rupert.

'There's nothing on the island really,' said Hugo.

'What?!' said Oliver Muddle. 'Are you sure you didn't miss anything?'

'Well, you could always go ashore and see for yourself,' said Walter. 'I mean, you'd have to fight off swarms of two-headed crocodiles, but I'm sure that wouldn't deter such an intrepid sailor.'

In the end Seaman Muddle decided he believed Walter's story. In fact, all the crew agreed that there probably wasn't anything very interesting on the island. There was certainly no need to go ashore to check it out.

But Rupert was getting angry. His face was bright purple and veins were standing out on his neck. 'I can't believe it. How can there possibly be an island with nothing on it? Where's my coconut? I told you to bring me back something like a coconut.'

'Ah yes!' said Hugo, rummaging in his satchel. 'There's nothing quite like a coconut on the island. But I did bring you this.'

Rupert studied the item Hugo was holding up. It was the size of a fist. It was brown and lumpy and covered in mud. 'What is it?' he said.

'It's a patata,' said Hugo, grinning. 'You can bake it or boil it and mash it up.'

Rupert took the patata and turned it over in his hand.

'Do you honestly expect me to present this revolting item, which seems to be covered in some sort of strange violet sand, to the King of England and tell him to eat it? He'd have my head on a platter.' With a huff of utter despair Rupert tossed the patata over his shoulder. It sailed over the side of the boat and plopped into the sea below.

Rupert climbed up to the rear deck to address his crew.

'Right, men. There's nothing on this island. Supplies are running low so we must head back to England.' He pointed at the horizon. 'We haven't discovered any-thing of note, but let's not think of this voyage as a failure. Think of it more as a fruitless exercise. A waste of time, if you like.'

The sailors looked at each other and frowned.

'What I am trying to say,' he continued, 'is that you are all fine sailors – even you, Muddle. We have bonded as a crew and put the small matter of the mutiny behind us. And I for one am proud to say that you are all beneath me. I mean, I'm your superior. I mean, I'm proud that you are my crew.'

As he bumbled on, Hawkeye climbed the rigging and Rockford raised the anchor.

Hugo and Walter stood at the back of the boat. Kramer waved from the ocean, his mouths curled into broad toothy grins.

Hugo slipped his hands into his pockets and yelped as he felt something warm and furry against his knuckles. Savage's head popped out of his pocket.

'Savage!' Hugo whispered. 'I'd forgotten you were in there.'

'I was just lying low for a while,' said Savage, blinking as he peered around. 'So this is the ship I've heard so much about?'

'We've just set sail,' said Hugo. 'Don't be upset, but we're on our way to England.'

'Upset? Who's upset?' said Savage. 'I hear that the world is full of exciting new places to explore. Naturally I'll miss Pigasus and the others, but I wouldn't have missed this adventure for the world!'

Hugo realized that he had a little furry stowaway on his hands, and smiled.

The three friends watched the fog bank around the island recede into the distance. The sea licked gently at the side of the boat. The air was warm and salty.

'Do you think anyone will ever visit the island again?' said Hugo.

'I shouldn't think so,' said Walter. 'At least, not for a very long time.'

'Where shall we go on our next expedition?'

'Wherever there's a new map to be made, I expect,' said Walter, moustache twitching. 'But I want you to promise me one thing, Hugo: next time we go off on an adventure, you have to try to stay out of danger.'

'Well,' said Hugo, giving his uncle a gap-toothed smile, 'I'll do my best.'

THE MAPMAKER'S MONSTERS

VAMPANTHER ATTACK!

Rob Stevens

Hugo and Savage are back, with more maps,
more monsters and more mayhem!

In their second adventure they travel to the
unchartered mountains of deepest Transylvania,
where nothing is as it seems. Will Crystal the
fortune-telling cat help them defeat the evil
vampanther lord – before it's too late?

Don't miss this fang-tastic book, coming in July 2009

BILLY BONES

a tale from the secrets closet

christopher lincoln

Everyone has a skeleton or two in their closet . . .

Hidden away under the stairs, Billy Bones the skeleton boy is just getting to grips with the rules of secret keeping:

1) It takes more energy to keep a secret than to share a secret.

2) The longer a secret remains a secret, the more energy it builds.

And, most importantly . . .

3) If a certain secret is exposed, it will cause a TERRIBLE explosion!

'Guaranteed to tickle the funny bone' - Lovereading4kids.co.uk